The Price of Valour

a novel by Dwight Purdy

✦

Published by the author
Elgin, Ontario
2005

✦

Library and Archives Canada Cataloguing in Publication

Purdy, Dwight, 1946-2005

The price of valour : a novel / by Dwight Purdy.

ISBN 0-9739320-0-7

1. World War, 1914-1918--Fiction. I. Title.

PS8631.U74P75 2005 C813'.6 C2005-906384-X

Cover Image:
Background - Jessica Bortnak
Illustrations - Raven Chartrand-Hunter

Printed and bound in Canada

Dwight Purdy
Elgin, ON

1 2 3 4 5 6 10 09 08 07 06 05

✦

In memory of my father,
an Ottawa boy of Irish descent
who served his country in a later war

✦

Author's Note

At the time of the First World War, Britain and her Dominions used the imperial system of measurement, while Germany employed the metric system. For the sake of simplicity, distances and weights are expressed throughout the novel in metric values.

Newsy Lalonde, Joe Malone, Gordon Flowerdew, Fred Harvey, Reginald Longley, Wilfred Hazel, George Henderson and Eddie Gerard were real people; the remaining characters are fictional. The Empire Hotel is also the author's creation.

The Price of Valour

by Dwight Purdy ✦

✦

We know it today as the First World War. Those who lived through it called it the Great War. For them, it was the defining event of their lives.

Its immediate cause was an act of terrorism. On June 28, 1914, an assassin shot and killed two members of the Austrian royal family. Their deaths sparked a chain of events that soon engulfed Europe in war. On one side were Germany and Austria-Hungary. Opposed to these central European states were Russia to the east and France and Britain to the west.

The fighting began in early August. By the spring of 1915, there was no prospect of peace in sight.

✦

Chapter 1

May 7, 1915

Rose Pearce found it hard to believe that something evil could be lurking beneath the gentle waves, ready to do the *Lusitania* harm. From the ship's promenade deck, fifteen metres above the waterline, the dark blue Celtic Sea, sparkling under the midday sun, looked so peaceful. Standing at the railing, Rose turned her gaze to the coastline of Ireland, now visible on the horizon. From below came the reassuring throb of the British liner's powerful engines. By this time tomorrow, she told herself, we'll be safely docked in Liverpool.

Rose just wished that Mary would share her confidence. She glanced at the older woman standing at her elbow. Mary Kincaid was travelling alone with her two young children to be closer to her husband, a Canadian soldier serving in France. Her younger child, a four-year-old boy named James, had been seasick for most of the voyage. Added to the burden of caring for her son was the constant worry that the *Lusitania* might be attacked by a German submarine.

Rose decided to try again to reassure her Canadian friend. "Surely, Mary, a ship carrying civilians isn't in danger."

"I wish I could believe that, Rose. But I don't trust those black-hearted Huns, not for a minute. Last month they used poison gas against Canadian soldiers at Ypres. They'd not think twice about sending this ship to the bottom with innocent women and children on board."

Mary's words sent a shiver up Rose's spine. She recalled an illustration in a history textbook of a fierce-looking barbarian on horseback. The Huns, her teacher explained, had struck terror in the hearts of their enemies by showing their victims no mercy. Rose had always thought of Germans as a civilized people. It seemed incredible to her that they should be now branded with such a horrid name.

"Had I known about the German threat before we boarded the *Lusitania,*" Mary continued, "I'd have cancelled our tickets and booked passage on an American ship."

Rose remembered the warning that appeared in the newspaper the morning the *Lusitania* set sail from New York. In a notice, printed on the same page as an advertisement announcing the liner's departure, the German embassy in Washington had warned transatlantic travellers that British ships entering British coastal waters ran the risk of being torpedoed by German submarines.

Mary never saw the notice. But Rose's grandfather had. "It's just a bluff," he'd said to Rose that morning on the New York pier where the *Lusitania* was berthed. "The Germans will never harm the *Lusy* with so many Americans on board. Keeping the United States neutral is in their best interests. You've no need to worry."

Rose trusted her grandfather's judgement. He'd never been wrong before. If only he were here now, she wished. He would know what to say.

Rose turned her head and looked fondly at Mary's children, seated together on a deck chair behind them. The older one, a ten-year-old girl named Liza, was reading to James from a storybook. The boy's face was deathly white. Only that morning had he been finally able to keep some food down after days of terrible vomiting that had left his small body weak and exhausted.

"You put on a very brave face for them, Mary."

"A soldier's wife learns to hide her fear."

Liza looked up from the book. "James's getting sleepy, Momma," she said.

"I'll take him for his nap in a moment," her mother answered.

Rose and Liza exchanged smiles.

"I must thank you, Rose," Mary said, "for all the time you've spent with Liza. Looking after James has been a full-time job."

"Liza's a delightful child, Mary."

"Well, I'd better tend to my son. Would you mind again...?"

"Not at all. I was about to suggest to Liza that we go to the verandah café for an ice cream."

"You spoil that girl."

"She's become the sister I never had."

"Rose." The gravity in Mary's voice was unmistakable. "If something should happen..."

"You needn't worry, Mary. I'll take good care of Liza."

The friendship between Rose and Liza had started in the ship's verandah café the second day out of New York. While her mother was busy with James, Liza had wandered off from their second-class cabin to explore the *Lusitania* on her own. Unnoticed, she entered the part of the ship reserved for first-class passengers. It wasn't until she appeared in the café, inquiring about an ice cream, that she was discovered. Liza Kincaid neither dressed nor spoke like a child of the well-to-do.

Seated alone at one of the tables, Rose had noticed Liza immediately. It wasn't her plain clothing that caught Rose's eye, but rather the look of pure wonderment on her face. When the steward took Liza's hand to escort her out, Rose intervened. "This young lady is my guest," she said. "I'll see to it that she's returned to her parents. But first I want you to bring her the biggest banana split on the menu." From that moment the two became inseparable.

✦

"Today you're going to have to earn your ice cream treat, Liza," Rose said as they watched Mary carry James off to her cabin.

Liza looked puzzled. "How, Rose?"

Rose smiled. "By proving me to be a good teacher."

"The way your grandfather was to you?"

"Exactly."

On their walks about the *Lusitania*, Rose had taught Liza many of the things she had learned about ships from her grandfather, a retired New England sea captain.

"Are you ready?" Rose asked.

"Ready!" Liza replied, barely able to contain her excitement.

"Here's your first question. We're facing the front end of the *Lusitania*. What's that part of the ship called?"

"The bow!"

"And the back end?"

"The stern!"

"And what's this side of the ship called?"

"Port!"

"And the other side, to our right?"

"Starboard!"

"And what's that above us?"

"The bridge!"

"And who's on the bridge?"

"Captain Turner!"

"Good for you, Liza!"

The young girl's face was wreathed in a smile.

"And now here's a bonus question for an extra scoop of ice cream. What type of ship did my grandfather sail?"

The smile turned quickly to a frown as Liza searched her brain for the answer. Then her eyes lit up. "A clipper ship!" she exclaimed.

"Correct!" Rose laughed and gave her young friend a hug. "We'll make a sailor of you yet."

Liza beamed with pride.

The café was located near the Lusitania's stern. On their way, Rose and Liza passed two men who tipped their hats and bid them a good afternoon. Farther along, they stopped and chatted briefly with two American nurses who, like Rose, were travelling to France to work at the American Red Cross hospital in Paris.

"Would you like to be a nurse, Rose?" Liza asked as they moved on.

"Perhaps one day, Liza. It takes many years to train to be a nurse. I'd rather do something right now to help France. That's why I accepted a clerical position at the hospital."

"But Momma says your country isn't at war. Why are you helping the French?"

Rose smiled at the young girl's inquisitiveness. Liza reminded her so much of herself when she was Liza's age.

"Some Americans," she explained, "disagree with our government's decision to stay neutral. France has a special place in our hearts. The French helped us win our revolution. It just seems like the right thing to do."

Just then their attention was drawn to an elderly man and a young boy standing at the railing. The man was pointing to the Irish coast. "That's the lighthouse on the Old Head of Kinsale," he explained to the boy. "I was born not far from there."

"Why is it called a 'head', Grandpa?" the boy asked.

"Well, 'tis like a big, long finger of rock that juts out from the mainland into the sea."

"Then why isn't it called the 'Old Finger of Kinsale'?"

The old man chuckled. The touching scene

reminded Rose of the many happy times she'd spent as a girl with her own grandfather. "You'll never guess, Liza, what my grandfather gave me for my sixteenth birthday."

"Tell me, please," the young girl said, her interest piqued.

"He took me around the world on his clipper ship. We visited exotic places like the African Gold Coast and the East Indies and China. Even though it was almost five years ago, I remember it like it was yesterday. It was an adventure — "

A sound, like a thud, stopped Rose in mid-sentence.

"Did you hear — ?"

A resounding BANG! drowned out the rest of Rose's question. Beneath her feet the deck shuddered.

"What was that, Rose?" The joy in Liza's voice was suddenly replaced by fear.

Rose forced herself to stay calm. "I'm not sure."

She quickly surveyed the faces of nearby passengers. Unbelievably, some seemed unaware that anything had happened. Others, however, showed concern.

"The deck! It's tilting!" a woman exclaimed.

The list, Rose quickly noted, was to starboard. There was something else that alarmed her even more: the *Lusitania*'s bow had dipped slightly into the water. Her stomach knotted as her brain quickly made sense of what had happened. A torpedo had struck somewhere forward on the starboard side of the ship.

At that moment a memory flashed through Rose's mind of a young girl shivering in the cold water of Cape Cod Bay as she tried to right her small sailboat. From the shore a man called out words of encouragement.

Don't panic, Rose. Keep your wits about you. You know what to do.

I'm trying, Granddad, I'm trying.

"We should find Momma and James." Liza's words jolted Rose back to the present.

Rose placed her hands on the young girl's shoulders. "Your mother will take good care of James. You must trust me, Liza, and do as I say."

Liza managed a weak smile. "I do trust you, Rose."

An Englishman standing nearby asked for everyone's attention. "There's no need to worry," he said calmly. "The *Lusy*'s unsinkable. Her watertight compartments will keep her afloat. As you can see, she's still underway. I am sure Captain Turner plans to bring her close to the Irish coast and beach her."

Rose stared at him in disbelief. In the few minutes since the explosion, the list had increased dramatically and the bow had settled even more. The captain must order full speed astern. Otherwise, Rose concluded, the *Lusitania* was going to plough right into the sea, long before she reached the Irish coast.

"I disagree with you, sir," Rose said to the Englishman. "I believe we're in serious danger." Her next words were addressed to the larger group. "You should all fetch your life belts and get to the boat deck as quickly as possible."

One woman gasped; another began to cry.

"Nonsense, you foolish girl," the Englishman snapped. "Shame on you for alarming everyone unnecessarily."

Rose ignored him. Taking Liza by the hand, she walked quickly to a nearby companionway. The *Lusitania*, she was convinced, was doomed. What these people did was up to them. All that mattered now was keeping her promise to Mary Kincaid.

"Where are we going, Rose?" Liza asked.

"To my cabin to get you my lifebelt." Rose's stateroom in first class was much closer than Mary's cabin in second class. "We don't have much time."

The list had tipped the stairs of the companionway. Climbing them was frustratingly slow. From deep within the hull came the moaning and screeching of metal under violent stress. Rose gripped Liza's hand more firmly. "Faster," she urged. "We must move faster."

By the time Rose and Liza, who was wearing Rose's lifebelt, reached the grand lobby on the boat deck, panic had seized the *Lusitania*'s passengers in its icy grip. Frantic men, women and children were pushing towards the exits. Above their shouts and cries could be heard the terrifying screams of those who had been trapped in the elevators when the ship's electrical power shut down.

Rose felt her courage slipping way.

Stay calm, Rose.

I'm trying, Granddad! I'm trying!

From the moment of the explosion Rose knew what she had to do. Her grandfather had told her often enough.

A sinking ship creates a swirling vortex that will suck you under, Rose. Make sure you get well clear.

But how, Granddad? How?

Rose knew that the heavy list would make the lifeboats useless. The port-side boats would swing in towards the ship, making it impossible for the davits to lower them. And the starboard ones would swing away from the ship, making them difficult to board.

How?

Rose felt a tug on her sleeve. It was Liza. With her other hand she was pointing to a woman and a small boy standing near the reception desk. "Look at their lifebelts!"

Rose immediately saw the problem. She rushed towards the woman, shouting, "Madam! Madam!" to get her attention.

"I'm looking for my husband," the woman cried out. "He told me to meet him here."

"Madam," Rose interrupted, "your lifebelts are on upside down!"

"It should be like mine," Liza gently explained to the boy who was fighting back tears. "Here, I'll help you change it."

Rose followed Liza's example and helped the woman put her lifebelt on correctly.

"Where's your lifebelt?" the woman asked Rose.

"I'll be all right. I'm a good swimmer."

The woman took Rose's hand. "God be with you," she said, and then she turned away to look for her husband.

Rose took Liza in her arms and hugged her tightly. "You're a brave girl, Liza. You may well have saved their lives."

"Rose, I'm a good swimmer, too. My poppa taught me."

"He did! I never thought … Oh, Liza, that changes everything!" Rose felt her courage returning. She quickly looked to the port doors. Most of the passengers in the lobby had chosen this exit. She understood why: the port boat deck, now the highest point on the *Lusitania*, would be the last part to sink. We'll be off the ship before that happens, Rose vowed to herself. She took Liza by the hand and said, "How about you and I go for a swim." Then she led her young friend down the sloping floor of the lobby to the starboard exit.

Rose shut her mind to the disorder and panic that surrounded them on the starboard boat deck. Instead, she quickly assessed the situation. The *Lusitania* continued its bow-first slide into the sea, which now reached as far as the bridge. And the list was now threatening to tip the ship over on its side. The great liner didn't have long before it disappeared beneath the waves.

Rose had been right about the lifeboats. Suspended from their davits, they swung away from the ship. Crew members struggled to pass women and children over the three-metre gap. The one closest to the water, boat Number 7, was just ten metres away. As a throng of people pushed forward to board it, an officer shouted, "Women and children only!"

Rose searched the water for the forward lifeboats whose davits were now submerged. One floated empty a short distance from the ship. But there was no sign of the others. There was no doubt now in Rose's mind that she'd made the right decision. "Liza, we must get rid of some of our clothing."

The young girl followed Rose's example. First she took off her shoes. Then she let her skirt drop to the deck and slipped out of her underskirt. Rose caught the disapproving look of a matronly woman out of the corner of her eye. The sight of the two of them in their knee-length drawers must have shocked others, but Rose never gave it a second thought.

A crew member suddenly appeared and swept Liza up in his arms. "Come on, luv," he said, "Number 7 has room for one more."

Rose grabbed hold of his arm. "Put her down!" she yelled.

The crewman looked over his shoulder in disbelief.

"Please," Rose said, "give her to me."

"Suit yourself, miss," he said as he set Liza back down the deck. Then he rushed off to find someone else to help.

Rose took Liza's hand and led her down the sloping deck to the railing where she peered over at the sea below. It had to be a ten-metre drop, she guessed, a daunting jump for even an experienced swimmer. But they had no choice, she told herself. They had to try. "Don't look down, Liza. Just hold on to the railing, while I climb over."

Once over, Rose perched precariously on the outer edge of the deck, clinging to the railing with one hand. She used her other hand to help Liza. The girl was trembling. "Remember, Liza, don't look down. Just grip my hand tightly and never let go. We'll jump on the count of three. Now take a big, deep breath and hold it. One … two… "

Mercifully, the water wasn't as cold as Rose expected. She kicked hard and pulled Liza with her to the surface. There they were accosted by the loud cracks of shattering wood and blood-curdling screams. Number 7 lifeboat was being crushed by its davits as the sinking *Lusitania* pulled it under. Treading water, Rose pulled Liza's face into her chest to shield her from the ghastly scene of carnage.

The empty lifeboat was about one hundred metres off the *Lusitania*'s stern, which was now out of the water, exposing the ship's gigantic propellers. Before attempting to reach it, Rose had a more immediate problem to deal with. The heavy list was threatening to tip the *Lusitania* on its side, bringing its massive superstructure, including the four colossal funnels still belching black smoke, down on top of them. "Liza, listen carefully to me. We must get as far away from the ship as we can. Now's the time to show me how well you can swim."

With a look of grim determination on her face, Liza began executing a perfect sidestroke. Her father had taught her well. Rose swam beside her, giving words of encouragement. At one point Rose glanced back to see a lifeboat, partially filled, safely in the water and moving away from the sinking ship. "You're doing well, Liza.

Keep it up. Help is on the way."

Finally, at a safe distance from the ship, Rose told Liza to rest and let the lifebelt do its job. The great liner was about to slip beneath the surface to its grave on the ocean floor. Hundreds of passengers still clung, without hope, to its stern decks. Their woeful cries were too much for Rose to bear. She broke down and wept. They were her first tears since the tragedy began.

Then it happened.

Without warning, the funnel closest to Rose and Liza wrenched free of its support cables and crashed into the sea just a short distance away. It was as if a giant empty bottle had suddenly been thrust into a mammoth tub of water. The surrounding water rushed through the opening to fill the empty space.

It happened so quickly that Rose had little time to react. "Take a deep breath, Liza!" she screamed as she watched Liza being sucked ahead of her into the mouth of the funnel. Inside, the heat expanded the cold seawater and spat it back out in bursts of black steam. Blackened from head to toe in grimy soot, Rose found herself once again floating in the water. Her eyes and throat burned from the acrid smoke. "Liza … Liza!" she called out in a hoarse voice that could barely be heard.

From behind her, Rose felt powerful hands under her arms lifting her from the water.

"No … please … Liza . . . I have to find her."

A man's voice spoke. "Sorry, ducks. Saw the two of ya sucked in, but only you came out. I'm afraid there's no hope."

"Oh, Liza …"

✦

The German plan in the summer of 1914 had been to defeat France first before turning against Russia. But the French, with British help, fought the Germans to a standstill. The line of battle separating the two sides became known as the Western Front. It stretched eight hundred kilometres from the English Channel to Switzerland.

To defend themselves, the opposing armies excavated trenches and underground dugouts and constructed machine gun emplacements and barbed wire obstacles. The ground separating these strong defences was called no man's land. It ranged from fifty metres to over a kilometre in width.

Over the next three-and-a-half years, both sides launched repeated attacks that made little or no gain at a cost of millions of casualties. These battles were fought by infantrymen and artillerymen. Cavalrymen, soldiers mounted on horses, were relegated to escorting prisoners to the rear and, as casualties mounted, to serving in the trenches.

Manning a section of the British trenches one hundred and fifty kilometres north of Paris in the winter of 1918 was a Canadian cavalry regiment called Lord Strathcona's Horse. At full strength, a cavalry regiment had five hundred men divided among three squadrons called "A", "B" and "C." Each squadron had four troops.

✦

Chapter 2

February 9, 1918

THE PATROL OF TWENTY SOLDIERS, FACES BLACKENED AND armed with rifles and grenades, assembled at Post Number 5 shortly before nine o'clock in the evening. The men were from 4th Troop, "C" Squadron, Lord Strathcona's Horse. The post was one of a series of strongly defended positions along the length of the firing trench, manned by the regiment's "B" Squadron.

The officer in charge of the patrol was Gordon Flowerdew. Born in England, Flowerdew had been farming in British Columbia when the war broke out. He'd served in the ranks before receiving his commission as a lieutenant. As the newly appointed commander of "C" Squadron, Lieutenant Flowerdew could have easily left the dangerous job of leading patrols to subordinates. However, the lieutenant was an officer who led by example.

Flowerdew's orders were to gather information about the German defences in this sector of the front line. His men were to use force only to defend themselves. At Flowerdew's signal, one of them jumped up on the firing step, climbed the remaining two metres to the top of the trench, and stepped over the parapet of stacked sandbags. He then quickly located and passed through the opening in the barbed wire that patrols used to enter and exit no man's land. There he waited for the rest of the patrol to catch up before moving on.

This man had the dangerous job of taking the point position. As the point man, he had the responsibility of making sure that the way ahead was clear of enemy patrols. Often he was the first to die. The point man on this night was Private Liam Cassidy.

To prepare himself for the patrol, Liam had spent time that afternoon studying a map of this part of no man's land. Fourteen hundred metres wide, its main features included two wooded areas, called Big Bill and Little Bill. Beyond Big Bill was an ancient quarry. From there it was a stone's throw to the German front line, a nice Sunday afternoon walk, if it weren't for the fact that he would be crossing the killing ground of the most brutal war in history. As he now headed towards Big Bill, Liam swore he could feel the presence of ghosts, the ghosts of the thousands of men whose blood had stained the ground on which he walked.

Halfway to the woods, the wind began to shift and grow stronger. Liam glanced skyward. Would the cloud cover hold? he wondered. The light of the moon would make it easier to keep his bearings, but it would also increase his chances of discovery. At least there was no snow on the ground. Against a white background, it was hard for a man to conceal himself.

What bothered Liam even more was the absence of German flares. That could only mean one thing: an enemy patrol had to be out there somewhere. But where? Maybe ahead of them at Big Bill or the quarry, waiting in ambush, or moving in behind them, cutting off their retreat. Dwelling on such thoughts was pointless, and Liam quickly pushed them from his mind.

It took thirty minutes to reach Big Bill. To Liam's relief, it was unoccupied. Soldiers called these pitiful stands of trees, shattered by shellfire, ghost woods. As he waited for the rest of the patrol to arrive, Liam allowed his mind to drift for a moment back to happier times when he was a boy hunting deer in the forests near Ottawa. Big Bill had witnessed killing on a more horrific scale.

Following the plan, the main body of the patrol remained at Big Bill, while Liam led Flowerdew and two other men to the quarry. Accompanying the lieutenant were Alex MacNeil and John Latimer.

Alex was Liam's closest friend. They had helped each other out of more than one tight spot. Not even a competition that had placed Liam just ahead of Alex as the top marksman in the regiment could weaken the bond of their friendship. Liam trusted the Scottish-born Albertan with his life.

He couldn't say the same for John Latimer. This was John's first patrol, and Liam wondered how he would hold up if they ran into trouble. In their dugout that afternoon, John had "gotten the wind up", the army's expression for showing fear. Nothing anyone said or did helped him to loosen up.

In the end, they had left John alone to face whatever private demons were tormenting him. They knew his choices were no choices at all. John could have said he was too sick to go on patrol, but no one would have believed him. Or he could have gone off somewhere and shot himself in the foot. All that would have got him was a long prison sentence with hard labour. Simply refusing to go was unthinkable. The army's regulations were clear: cowardice in the face of the enemy was a capital offence. That meant death by firing squad. When it came time for the patrol to set off, John was there, ready to do his duty.

Liam started out towards the quarry, the other three following about thirty metres behind. They were getting closer now to the German line, and Liam moved slowly, listening carefully for anything, a footstep, a whisper, a cough, that would reveal the presence of the enemy. No man's land was eerily quiet.

BOOM! BOOM! Liam's heart jumped into his throat as German artillery opened up two kilometres to his right. He stopped to watch the red hot shells streaking across the black sky. Some Tommies, he told himself, were in for a long night.

As he continued towards the quarry, Liam now had to concentrate on what he could see rather than hear. Turning his head slowly from side to side, he searched the shadows for the slightest movement. In the sky overhead, he noticed blotches of light appearing in the thinning cloud cover. By the time he reached the quarry, the moon had broken through, bathing the war-ravaged landscape in a soft, pale light. Liam moved to the edge of the quarry and looked in.

There was no sign of the enemy.

Something, however, caught his attention. Reflecting the moonlight was a large pool of water that collected at the bottom of the quarry during the autumn rains. The freezing temperatures had turned it into a perfect sheet of ice, like the frozen ponds he'd played hockey on as a boy. Just then, the moon disappeared behind a cloud, and the ice-covered pool was swallowed up in the darkness. Soon the others arrived, and it was back to the business of war.

Lieutenant Flowerdew used hand signals to explain what he wanted to do next. Liam was to come with him for a closer look at the German wire, while Alex and John stayed at the quarry to provide cover. With the clouds breaking up, another officer might have called it quits and headed home, but not the lieutenant. Nothing seemed to deter him from doing his duty. Liam prayed that the cloud cover would hold a bit longer and followed Flowerdew towards the German line.

At that moment, the German guns fell silent, and once more no man's land was deadly quiet. The Germans were bound to have listening posts in front of their barbed wire. With each step Liam knew that the slightest noise he made could unleash a hail of bullets in his direction.

They had gone about halfway when the sky started to brighten. Moments later the moon reappeared through a break in the clouds. Liam froze in his tracks, willing every part of his body to remain still. Just ahead he could see the lieutenant, standing motionless. A short distance beyond him, shimmering in the moonlight, were strands of frost-covered barbed wire — German barbed wire. Liam felt his heart would explode. One thought burned a hole through his brain: not far away a German machine gunner was about to cut him to pieces. He was going to die.

But nothing happened.

For several minutes the two men stood like statues. Then the lieutenant started to move. Slowly he walked up to the barbed wire and looked around. It was then that Liam understood. The Germans didn't have enough soldiers to man fully this part of their front line. Like the Strathconas, they were relying on outposts. This section of the German firing trench was empty.

The lieutenant had obviously reached the same conclusion. He turned and walked back towards Liam. "I think we can call it a night, Private," he whispered.

Chapter 3

HOME FOR LIAM CASSIDY WAS AN UNDERGROUND shelter three metres high and five metres square. It was one of a honeycomb of dugouts that had been excavated along the support trench, a hundred metres behind the firing line.

Liam shared his dugout with five other men, including Alex MacNeil and John Latimer. They slept in bunks of rough timber and wire mesh, erected along the side walls. At the rear of the dugout was a small coal-burning stove, vented up to ground level. Covering the entrance was a piece of heavy burlap to keep out enemy gas.

Lying in his bunk, Liam could hear rats scurrying about the dugout floor. The stomach-turning odour of unwashed bodies was one thing. He could even put up with the lice that infested his body and clothes. But the rats terrified him. Feasting on the corpses that littered the battlefield, they had grown as big as cats. He'd heard stories of some even attacking men while they slept.

Now Liam could look forward to ten vermin-free days. On their return from the patrol, the troop sergeant had greeted him with the news that his leave orders had been sent up from regimental headquarters.

"You'll miss out on gettin' your medal," Alex had kidded him. For days the rumour had been circulating that headquarters was planning a raid on the German lines. What Lieutenant Flowerdew had learned that night about their defences would prove invaluable in planning such an operation.

"You can be the war hero," Liam had retorted. "I'm goin' to put as much distance between me and this hell-hole as I can."

Now, in the bunk above, Alex snored softly, oblivious to the danger of the rats. His rum ration had taken effect. There was, however, no rum in Liam's stomach to calm his nerves. As always, he'd been tempted when the sergeant showed up after the patrol with the earthenware jug labelled "Special Ration Distribution." But a promise to his mother was a promise to be kept. Now his nervous system, still recovering from the excitement of the patrol, denied the rest of his body the sleep it so desperately needed.

Liam reached into one of the breast pockets of his tunic and pulled out an envelope. Inside was a recent letter from his sister. Maggie's other letters, as well as photographs of her and their mother, had been lost during the fighting the previous November. This letter was the only link he had to his family, to his hockey career with the Ottawa Senators, to his peaceful, contented life in Le Breton Flats, the Ottawa neighbourhood where he lived.

Maggie had opened the letter with the news of the birth in January of her third child, her first boy. Her husband, Seamus, had been away at the time, working in one of the Ottawa valley's many lumber camps. Seamus was a giant of a man with a kind heart and a gentle nature. Liam knew the birth of a son would bring him great joy.

Liam was relieved to learn from Maggie that their mother was still managing in his absence. In her retirement Liam had been her sole means of support. A cheque from the army, in the amount of half his pay, continued to arrive monthly, and someone from the hockey club brought her some coal and firewood and a box of groceries once a week.

Liam tried to picture his mother, sitting in her rocking chair in the kitchen of the two-storey row house she rented on Queen Street West. Le Breton Flats was her home. It was where she belonged. The day after she buried her husband, just two weeks after the Great Fire of 1900 destroyed the Flats, including their row house on nearby Broad Street, she'd promised Maggie and Liam that one day they would return. It was, she told them, what their father would have wanted.

In the years that followed, they'd moved from place to place, mostly rooming houses in the city's east end.

To support herself and her two children, Maeve Cassidy worked six days a week as a scullery maid in the kitchen of the Russell House, a hotel on Elgin Street. At night she took in sewing for a local tailor.

Then one day, six years after the fire, his mother came home from work with the news that they'd be moving again. Seeing the disappointment on Maggie's face, she quickly added, "There's no reason to be sad, child. This'll be our last move. Today, I found us a house in the Flats." Two weeks later they moved their few belongings into Number 126, Queen Street West. His mother had kept her promise.

Liam returned the envelope to the safety of his pocket. Would he survive the war, he wondered, to see his mother and sister again? Would he have the chance to teach his new nephew how to skate? Would he ever play in the new league that Maggie described in her letter? They called it the National Hockey League. It had started the previous November with four teams: the Senators, the Toronto Arenas, and two Montreal teams, the Wanderers and the Canadiens. When a fire destroyed the Wanderers' rink, the league was reduced to three teams. By Christmas, the Canadiens, led by Joe Malone and Newsy Lalonde, were in first place.

Newsy Lalonde.

Liam raised his hand to his face and ran a finger over an ugly scar above his right eye. It had taken twelve stitches to close the wound opened by Lalonde's stick that December night in 1913. "Welcome to the big league, Mick," Lalonde had snarled, standing over Liam who was on his hands and knees, his blood spattering the ice beneath his face.

Ice.

Liam recalled the ice-covered pond at the bottom of the quarry in no man's land. He pictured himself on skates, gliding over the smooth, glassy surface, pushing a puck ahead of him with his hockey stick.

Thinking about ice, he finally drifted into sleep …

The ice covering the lower part of the walls contrasted grotesquely with the blackened stone above that had been out of reach of the fire hoses. That's what had struck Liam the most when he saw the fire-gutted Parliament Buildings that wintry Ottawa morning in 1916. The temperature had been so cold during the night that the jets of water from the hoses had frozen on the walls before they could reach the raging inferno that had destroyed everything inside.

Liam had joined the large crowd that stood in stunned silence, staring at the smoldering remains of the Gothic structure that, just the day before, had housed Canada's government. A steam-driven pumper, belching smoke from its boiler, continued to push water through hoses that snaked across the snow-covered grounds to crews of firemen who directed it through broken windows. The smoke-filled air stung the nostrils and brought tears to the eyes of many of the onlookers.

Mixed with these were tears of sadness. News had spread quickly about the loss of life in the fire. "Two women they know of for sure," Liam heard someone say.

"Bloody murderers," said another. "When they find the Huns who did this, they should hang 'em on the spot. Don't deserve a trial if you ask me."

Liam turned to an elderly man standing beside him. "What's he talkin' about?"

"People're saying it was sabotage," the man replied. "Claim German spies started the fire."

Liam shook his head in disbelief. It never ceased to

amaze him how the war had turned normally sensible people into blithering idiots. His heart went out to the city's residents of German ancestry. Talk of enemy spies could only make life more difficult for them.

Was there proof that the fire had been set on purpose? He wanted to ask the man, but thought better of it. Instead, he said, "More likely some politician fell asleep while he was smokin' his big cigar." Deciding he had seen and heard enough, Liam turned to make his way out of the crowd.

In his path stood a well-dressed woman.

"Excuse me, ma'am," he said.

But the woman stood her ground.

When he started to go around her, she moved to block his way.

Liam looked at her, expecting some kind of explanation for her strange behaviour. What he saw took him aback. Her skin was deathly pale and drawn tightly over her cheekbones. Dark shadows underlined her eyes, which seemed almost lifeless. It took a moment for Liam to realize that she was quite young, probably about his age.

"I despise you," she said.

Her words struck him like a punch to the face. Surely, she can't be speaking to me, Liam thought. She must've mistaken me for someone else.

"Do I know you, ma'am?"

"No, you do not. However, I know who you are. You're Liam Cassidy," she said contemptuously, "the professional hockey player."

"That's right. Is there somethin' I can do for you?"

By this time the encounter had attracted the attention of a number of people standing nearby.

"What you can do for me, Mr. Cassidy, is explain why a young, able-bodied man like yourself is not in

France fighting to defeat the barbarians responsible for this cowardly act." She pointed to the smoldering Parliament Buildings.

Liam tried to check the anger he could feel building up inside him. He had been brought up to treat women with respect, but this one had gone too far. "I would say that's none of your business."

"Oh, but it is my business, Mr. Cassidy. You see, my husband, a brave and honourable man, has given his life in this war so that men like you can go about living your lives in safety."

"I'm sorry for your loss, but — "

"I don't want your sympathy, Mr. Cassidy. What I wish is that you do your duty as a man. Until that time, you can wear this symbol of your cowardice."

With that, she pulled a white feather from her pocket and stuck it into the buttonhole of his coat lapel.

Liam sat up in his bunk, his heart racing, his body drenched in a cold sweat.

Coward.

It ranked right up there with thief or murderer as the worst thing to call a man.

Liam was up well before daybreak, packing his kit bag. Movement to and from the front line was restricted to the cover of darkness, and he planned to be long gone when the sun rose. The only other man in the dugout who was awake was John Latimer. John sat on the edge of his bunk, staring at a photograph he held in his right hand.

Liam decided to strike up a conversation. "Your sweetheart?" Liam asked.

"My fiancée," John replied. "We plan to be married when the war's over. I'll be takin' over the family farm.

It should provide us with a good life."

"Where's home?"

John returned the photograph to a breast pocket in his tunic. "Nova Scotia," he said. "A town called Middleton, near the Bay of Fundy."

Liam tightened the drawstrings of his kit bag. "You did a good job last night on patrol."

John forced a smile. "It was all I could do to keep my fear under control."

"You're no different from the rest of us, John. Only a fool says he's not afraid."

"How do you do it, Liam … overcome your fear, that is?"

Liam gave a shrug. "I just keep tellin' meself not to let me mates down. It's somethin' I learned playin' hockey."

Just then Alex MacNeil rolled over on his back. "How's a man to sleep," he growled, "with all this infernal jabber!"

Liam laughed as he picked up his rifle and kit bag. "See you in couple of weeks, you Scottish ox," he said as headed for the dugout door.

"Give all those London lasses a kiss for me!" Alex shouted after him. Then he rolled over and went back to sleep.

Liam reported to the troop sergeant who gave him permission to leave the support trench. Then he set out for the communication trench that connected to the road that led to the reserve area. He hadn't gone far when, without warning, it happened. A heavy-calibre German shell, the type Canadians called a coal box, slammed into the support trench not fifteen metres from the dugout Liam had just left. The explosion demolished a whole section of the trench, sending a huge cloud of black smoke into the air. The concussion lifted

Liam off his feet and sent him sprawling to the bottom of the communication trench. With the ringing in his ears, he could barely hear the shouts: "Stretcher-bearers! On the double!" Liam struggled to his feet and ran back to help.

In the support trench he found a dozen men, stumbling about, coughing and retching from the explosive's acrid fumes. Among them was Alex MacNeil, his hair and clothes dishevelled and caked in dirt, blood streaming from his nostrils.

Liam quickly learned that his dugout, with its reinforced ceiling of wooden beams, had survived the shelling. John Latimer, however, hadn't been so lucky. Just before the shell hit, John had left the dugout to use the latrine.

With shovels, they dug for over an hour hoping to find John buried alive. But all they uncovered was one of his boots. His foot was still in it.

Chapter 4

February 11, 1918

LIAM JOINED A GROUP OF BRITISH SOLDIERS, SHIVERING in the damp cold as they waited on the pier to board the channel steamer. Like the others, Liam carried a full pack on his back and a Lee Enfield rifle slung over his shoulder. Even away from the battlefield, a soldier was burdened with the tools of his trade.

About them the French port of Boulogne buzzed with activity. Nearby stevedores unloaded munitions from a freighter. In the harbour a troopship from Britain sounded its siren to announce its arrival. Even this far from the Western Front, fighting a war was still a round-the-clock undertaking.

"Been long since you were in Blighty?"

The question came from the Tommy they called Harry.

"Over a year," Liam answered.

Someone else cursed the cold.

"Oh, stop your complainin', Bert," said Harry. "You'll be 'ome soon and that wife of yours'll warm you up quick enough."

Liam joined in the laughter. It helped to release some of the nervous energy that had built up inside him. Already it was the second day of his ten-day leave. He wouldn't reach London until late afternoon — and he could hardly wait.

Staying the night in Boulogne at a leave camp had meant one less day in London. It was a decision Liam hoped he wouldn't regret. The one consolation was the camp had provided the first hot bath he'd had in months. That, together with a change of underwear and a fumigated uniform, made him feel almost human again. Harry had obviously decided to wait until he crossed the Channel before he cleaned himself up. The smell of him made Liam think of the trenches, something he wanted desperately to put out of his mind.

Finally, the soldiers were told they could board the steamer. They filed up the gangplank to the main deck and headed to the passenger cabin, all except Liam, who chose instead to remain on deck. Harry called after him. "Are you daft, lad? Com'in with us where it's warm."

"Canucks're built to take the cold weather," Liam answered. "I'll join you in a minute."

Liam headed towards the stern, the deck beneath his feet vibrating as the engine increased speed. Slowly, the steamer pulled away from the pier and headed out of the harbour. Overwhelmed by a sudden bout of homesickness, he needed to be alone for a few minutes.

At the stern he stood, leaning against the railing, staring at the steamer's wake.

These British soldiers were so lucky. Within a day or two they would all be home with their families. Liam thought of his mother and his sister with her new baby. How his heart ached for home. As he looked up to see Boulogne and the military camps on the surrounding hills growing smaller in the distance, he wished he were seeing France for the last time. Damn this war! he cursed to himself, and turned to retrace his steps to the cabin entrance.

It was then that Liam saw her standing at the railing at the opposite end of the steamer, near the bow. Bundled up in her hat and winter coat, hands stuffed into the pockets, she stared into the distance, her head slowly rotating from side to side as if she were on watch. A female crew member? Liam quickly dismissed the thought as ridiculous. Then what was she doing out in this wretched weather? He shrugged his shoulders, opened the cabin door and went inside.

The cabin was crowded and noisy. But it didn't take Liam long to find Harry and the others. They were seated on benches sipping mugs of tea and munching on sandwiches they had purchased from the canteen located in the middle of the cabin. Harry called to him to join them. Liam answered with a wave. He found a place to store his pack and rifle and made his way to the canteen.

Minutes later, a mug of tea in hand, he'd forgotten about Harry. Instead, he made his way back to the cabin door and the main deck.

"Pardon me, miss. I thought you might appreciate somethin' to warm you up."

When the woman turned to face him, Liam held

out the mug of tea. She said nothing in response as if she hadn't heard a word he said. However, her eyes spoke volumes. What Liam saw in them, he had seen in the eyes of so many of his fellow soldiers. It was fear, raw fear.

"Tea's not me choice of beverage," he added. "But it's hot."

"Please forgive my rudeness." There was a tremor in her voice. "I was lost in thought." She pulled a hand from her coat pocket, took the mug by the handle and brought it to her lips, drinking in brief sips.

Liam noticed that three of her knuckles had been badly skinned and were just starting to heal over.

"You're very kind," she gasped, the hot tea burning her throat.

They both laughed. Her laughter was warm and genuine, and Liam loved it.

"Are you on leave?" she asked.

"Just ten days."

"I'm a bit more fortunate. I have two weeks," she replied, her face softening as she became more relaxed. "Do you have plans?"

What a lovely face it is, was all Liam could think.

"I asked if you had plans," she said, her expression changing to puzzlement.

"Sorry! It's me who should apologize now. Plans? Yeah, the usual. Headin' to the Big Smoke for the sights and a show. And you?"

The woman didn't answer. Instead, she pulled her other hand from its warm pocket and pointed out to sea. "Look," she said, her voice filled with alarm. In the distance Liam could see the wisps of smoke from another ship. As it drew closer, he recognized the profile of a warship.

"It's just the Royal Navy keepin' those German submarines at bay." Liam studied the ship more closely. "I wonder what kind she is."

"That's a destroyer, mate." They both turned their heads to find a member of the steamer's crew standing nearby, the pipe he was smoking in his hand. "And don't be foolin' yourself," he continued, "a torpedo'll send 'er to the bottom just as fast as it will this ol' tub." The crewman chuckled, returned his pipe to his mouth, and went off about his business.

The woman visibly trembled at the mention of the word torpedo. Then she turned away to resume her vigil. Not sure what to say, Liam tried the first thing that came into his head. "It's hard to imagine a boat that travels underwater and sinks large ships with a bomb that looks like a fish. This war sure's changin' the world, and definitely not for the better."

The woman made no reply.

Liam shrugged his shoulders. "Well, I should shove off." He turned and started walking towards the cabin door.

"Don't go." This time the fear was in her voice. "I would be very grateful if you stayed. My name is Rose Pearce."

"I'm Liam, Liam Cassidy."

"I'm pleased to meet you, Liam," Rose said, taking note of the badge on Liam's cap. "I see you're in the cavalry. And an expert with a rifle," she added, glancing down at the marksman badge on his left sleeve. It depicted two rifles, their barrels crossed.

"You know your military badges, Rose."

When she smiled this time, her teeth showed, perfect and white. "I see a lot of them in my line of work."

"And what line of work would that be?"

"I'm an ambulance driver for the Voluntary Aid Detachment."

"How'd that come about?"

Rose turned her head to the sea and looked off into the distance. "I came to France three years ago to work as a clerk at an American hospital near Paris. At the time it seemed exciting, but I soon grew tired of the routine. I'd remembered seeing a V.A.D. advertisement in the *Times* when I stopped over in London on my way to Paris. It said you had to be twenty-three to drive an ambulance. So last June, on my twenty-third birthday, I applied." She looked again at Liam and, with a smile, added, "And here I am."

"And your hand? What happened to it?"

"Oh, that," Rose held up her injured hand, an embarrassed look on her face. "I was a bit careless fixing a punctured tire," she explained. "Maintaining our own vehicles is one of our duties. Unfortunately, I can be a bit clumsy at times with a wrench." This time the laugh was forced. "I'm afraid I'm the target for quite a bit of teasing from some of the other girls."

But Liam didn't laugh. "I think you're very brave."

"Well, my work is not nearly as dangerous as yours, but I want to do what I can to help out."

"You've an accent I can't quite place, Rose, if you don't mind me askin'"

"I'm an American. From Cape Cod. A little town called Barnstable."

"Well, I'll be, a Yank. I met a Yank once. He owned the lumber mill where me dad worked."

"Was that in Canada?"

"Yeah, Ottawa."

"A Canadian with a hint of an Irish accent."

"Me mum and dad came from the old country. Had six kids. Only two of us survived, me and Maggie, a younger sister."

Just then the steamer's whistle sounded. The crewman reappeared. "Folkestone in fifteen minutes," he called out. They turned their heads towards the bow to see the English coastline looming in the distance.

"Well, I'd better fetch me kit," Liam said.

"I hope you enjoy your leave, Liam."

He nodded with a smile and started towards the cabin door.

"Liam," Rose called after him.

He stopped and looked back over his shoulder.

"I'm staying at the Empire Hotel in London. I'd like to see you again."

All Liam could think of was how glad he was he'd taken that hot bath the night before.

✦

Germany could never hope to win the war fighting on two fronts. In the east, Russia proved to be a resilient opponent. After suffering humiliating defeats in 1914 and 1915, the Russians recovered and won a major battle against the Austrians in 1916. Then, in April 1917, the United States declared war on Germany. American entry into the conflict promised to tip the scales on the Western Front in favour of Britain and France.

However, it would take a year or more for the Americans to train and ship their soldiers to Europe. There was still a chance to turn the war in Germany's favour. The opportunity came when Russia, weakened by heavy losses and political revolution, withdrew from the war in the late autumn of 1917. The Germans could now concentrate all their military strength in the west. The year 1918 brought Germany the hope of victory.

✦

Chapter 5

February 11, 1918

THE DISTANT THUNDER OF ARTILLERY INTERRUPTED DIETER Hannsen's morning walk on the Schlossberg, the small mountain that overlooked Freiburg, a university town in Germany's Black Forest. Most Freiburgers would have gone about their business. For them, the sounds of the Western Front, just sixty-five kilometres to the west, had long lost their novelty. Three-and-a-half years of war had a way of dulling the senses. Dieter, however, couldn't resist the urge to stop and listen. His was the curiosity of a professional. As a gunner in the German artillery, he took pride in being able to recognize guns by their sound when fired. What he heard now was the distinctive rumble of heavy artillery, but the guns were too far away to identify their type.

While serving on the Eastern Front, Dieter had seen for himself the destructive power of heavy guns. Whole villages and towns had been levelled to the ground. Even churches had been reduced to heaps of rubble. Church towers, often used by the enemy as observation posts, were a gunner's first targets.

Dieter's gaze shifted from the distant mountains to Freiburg's great cathedral in the valley just below him. Freiburg had suffered some damage from French air raids, but so far the cathedral had been spared. For this blessing, Dieter was thankful.

Churches in Germany had been required to give up their bells to provide badly needed metals for the war effort. But Freiburg's cathedral had managed to keep its original bell. Called the Hosanna, it was hung in 1258. At that moment, the Hosanna began to ring, calling Freiburg's faithful to morning mass. Dieter had lost track of the time. If he didn't hurry, he would be late.

The path down the mountain overlooked the Schwabentor, one of two medieval gates that separated Freiburg's old town from the surrounding modern suburbs. Painted on the outer wall of the gate was a picture of St. George, Freiburg's patron saint, with a slain dragon at his feet. What Dieter saw beneath the painting brought him to an abrupt halt. A woman was about to be robbed by two youths. He was too far away to call out a warning. All he could do was watch.

The woman had passed through the gate on her way out of the old town. One of the boys approached her from the front to distract her. The other came up from behind, snatched her handbag and shoved it inside his coat. The accomplice ran through the gate into the old town, while the thief sprinted across the street and headed for the set of stairs that led up to the base of the mountain.

Dieter quickly guessed the thief's plan: once up in the mountain, he would find a secluded spot in the forest to search the handbag for valuables. But first he had to get past Dieter. It wasn't long before he caught sight of the thief, running up the path about thirty metres below him. He looked about fourteen years of age. When he saw Dieter, the boy slowed down to a walk and tried to act nonchalantly. Just as he was about to go by, Dieter grabbed him by the arm. With his other hand, he reached inside the boy's coat and pulled out the handbag.

"Let me go!" the boy yelled as he tried to pull away. But Dieter's grip was too strong

"I found that on the street!"

"Don't lie to me. I saw you steal it. What would your father say if he knew his son was a thief?"

"What business is it of yours?" There was no sign

of remorse in the boy's eyes, only defiance. "And, anyway, my father was killed at the front. So what does it matter?"

"It matters to the rest of your family. You'll be no good to them, not to mention yourself, if you end up in prison one day."

The boy refused to answer, retreating instead behind a wall of sullenness. Part of Dieter wanted to haul the boy down to the police station. Juvenile delinquency had become a serious problem throughout Germany. The war had left many families without the firm, guiding hand of a father. At the same time, Dieter couldn't help feeling sympathy for the boy. How would I have turned out, Dieter wondered, had I lost my father at that age? "If I let you go, will you promise me to stay out of trouble?"

The boy looked down at his feet and nodded his head.

"Look at me and say it!"

The boy did as he was told. "I promise," he said in a more respectful tone.

"Then be off with you."

The boy started back down the path.

"Not that way. You'd better make yourself scarce for a while," Dieter said, pointing up the mountain.

As he watched the boy disappear up the path, Dieter wondered if he had made a mistake not turning him over to the police. Then, with a shrug, he turned to go. That's when he saw her, accompanied by a policeman, coming up the path. The woman looked about his age.

"St. George hasn't abandoned you," Dieter said to her as he gave her the handbag, "but I'm afraid the thief escaped."

The policeman accepted Dieter's explanation that the youth had veered off into the woods when he saw

Dieter approaching. In his haste to escape, he'd accidentally dropped the handbag. Already red-faced from the climb up the mountain, the stout, middle-aged constable took one look up into the woods and then headed back down the path, muttering something about "young derelicts".

"*Dankeschoen*, Dieter," the woman said. "I'm very grateful."

"You … you know my name," Dieter stammered.

"But you don't remember me," she replied, unable to hide her disappointment.

Dieter felt his face flush with embarrassment. "*Nein*, I'm afraid I don't."

"Well, I'll forgive you. It's been almost four years since we were introduced."

Dieter frantically searched his memory for a name.

"Lili Bloch," she said, extending her hand.

"*Ja*, of course, I remember now," Dieter exclaimed as he took her hand. "You're Friedrich Bloch's daughter. We met at the Conservatory recital the summer the war started." The pretty face of the fifteen-year-old girl he'd met that day was now pale and drawn. The food shortages had taken their toll.

"Karl," Lili said, "was one of my father's most gifted students."

Dieter's older brother had studied piano under Professor Bloch before training as a fighter pilot. Karl Hannsen had been killed over the Western Front just before Christmas.

"I cried," she continued, "when I read the news of Karl's death."

"And I was sorry, Lili, to hear about your parents." Professor Bloch and his wife had been killed the previous summer when a bomb struck their home during a French air raid.

"We've all suffered in this war, Dieter," Lili replied. "Germany's a nation in perpetual mourning."

"Your brother, Ernst, how's he?" Dieter didn't know Ernst Bloch personally but had idolized him as one of Freiburg's outstanding football players. The news that Ernst had lost a leg at the Battle of Verdun in 1916 had shocked the town's sports community.

"We live together in a small flat on Albert Strasse. We manage on his government pension and what I can earn giving piano lessons."

Dieter knew that couldn't be true. Even his father's university salary had failed to keep pace with Germany's soaring cost of living.

"You'll have to excuse me, Dieter. I'm already late for a lesson."

Dieter offered to walk with her. As they headed down the path, he suggested they get together later for a glass of wine. At first Lili declined, but Dieter persisted. "In another time I would have suggested coffee. But I can't stomach the stuff they're rationing now. They say it's made from tree bark."

He could see Lili's reserve starting to melt. "I can't remember," she said, "what real coffee tastes like."

"Then you'll accept my invitation."

"I don't think — "

"Surely you wouldn't disappoint a soldier home on leave?"

"Well, since you put it that way, you may call on me around eleven. We're at Number 12, the second floor."

"I'm looking forward to it."

Finally, a smile came. "It's the least I can do for my St. George."

Dieter thought he had become hardened to the sight of limbless men. Seeing Ernst Bloch, however, left him visibly shaken. The man in the doorway of the flat had once been a gifted athlete who brought cheering spectators to their feet with his lightning speed and brilliant dribbling. Now he supported himself on crutches, his right leg amputated above the knee.

Ernst seemed to sense his discomfort. "I'm getting fitted for a new prosthesis tomorrow," he explained. "In another few weeks I'll be back to looking normal."

Dieter felt ashamed for his indiscretion. "I apologize, Ernst. It's just that I remember you from another time."

"Well, those times are gone."

"I'm sorry."

"Don't be. I'm not. I'm alive, which is more than I can say for many of the lads I played with. Anyway, why don't you come in and have a seat." He pointed to two wooden chairs at a table covered by a well-worn oilcloth. "Lili'll be back shortly. She's just looking in on an elderly lady down the hall."

The flat was small, drab, and sparsely furnished. Dieter took one of the chairs while Ernst manoeuvered himself into the other. "It's not much," he apologized. "When I get a job, I hope I can provide us with something better."

Dieter understood his embarrassment. Like all middle-class Germans, Ernst Bloch had been raised to believe that respectability and material comfort were the rewards of hard work and thriftiness. Dieter wondered if those pre-war days, when everything seemed right with the world, were gone forever.

"This is for you and Lili," Dieter said, placing a package wrapped in newspaper on the table. "It's venison. I shot a deer in the forest north of the Titisee the third day of my leave. A local man butchered it for me in return for a share of the meat."

"Then I'm twice indebted to you, Dieter. Lili told me what happened earlier this morning."

"I just happened to be in the right place at the right time."

"I know just what you mean." Ernst paused, placing a hand on what was left of his right leg. "A French shell exploded within metres of my squad. Eight good men died. Only I survived. My parents, on the other hand, were unfortunate enough to be in the wrong place at the wrong time. Those French aviators could have hit any one of hundreds of houses in Freiburg." At this point, Ernst seemed to stare off into space, a haunted look in his eyes. His next words came in almost a whisper. "The random violence of war."

Dieter remembered stories of the Battle of Verdun, stories of men driven to mutiny and madness by the relentless shelling and endless carnage. In Ernst's eyes, Dieter believed he caught a brief glimpse of a man's soul, permanently scarred by the unspeakable horrors he had witnessed.

Suddenly, Ernst's mind returned to the present as quickly as it had left. "I see you're in the field artillery," he said, taking note of the scarlet piping and shoulder straps on Dieter's tunic.

Dieter nodded. "The seven-point-seven's our gun," he said, referring to Germany's 7.7-centimetre light field gun.

Ernst laughed. "You've a gunner's loud voice, Dieter. All you lads'll be stone deaf by the time this war's over."

Dieter smiled, thankful that the tone of the conversation had lightened. "The army turned me into a gunner when they found out I was good at mathematics." He went on to explain that he'd joined his regiment on the Eastern Front the previous summer but hadn't seen much action. When the Russian war effort collapsed, he'd been lucky enough to be given leave. In two days, he was to rejoin his regiment, which had been transferred to the Western Front to train for the anticipated German offensive in the spring.

Ernst seemed to be only half listening. By the time Dieter finished, Ernst's sombre mood had returned. "Our gunners were supposed to destroy the French defences at Verdun," he said. "The infantry were told it would be like a Sunday stroll through the park. Instead, we were chewed to pieces by French shelling and machine gun fire."

The criticism stung Dieter and left him at a loss for words. After an uncomfortable moment, Ernst spoke again, the bitterness now gone from his voice. "Please forgive my bad manners, Dieter. It's just that I've had hard time forgetting what happened. So many good men died. Some of them were friends. All for nothing. When it was all over, not one metre of ground had been gained from the enemy."

"This time things will be different," Dieter said. "The Russian surrender has freed up our soldiers in the east for the attack on the British and the French. We're certain to win."

"I hope you're right," Ernst replied. "If we don't defeat them before the Americans arrive, then all will be lost."

To Dieter, Ernst was a man who had aged before his time. He had to remind himself that Ernst was only a few years older than himself.

Just then the door opened and Lili entered the flat. "Sorry for being late," she explained. "Frau Schmidt wanted to talk. She's so lonely."

"Lili, look what Dieter brought us. Some venison."

Lili stared coldly at the package on the table. Then

she went to a nearby closet and took out a coat. As she put it on, she said, "I'm sorry, Dieter, but we can't accept your gift."

"Lili, you don't know what you're saying."

"You know how I feel, Ernst. Butcher shops haven't stocked venison for a year. The hunters have been keeping it for themselves." Then she looked at Dieter. "The man who sold you that is a black market profiteer. He should be arrested."

"I didn't buy it," Dieter said. "I shot it myself."

"You're a hunter?" Lili's cheeks went crimson.

"Not a very good one. But sometimes I get lucky."

Dieter could see Ernst shaking his head. "You'll have to forgive my sister, Dieter. Sometimes she gets carried away with her patriotism."

"Oh, Dieter, I feel so foolish. Please forgive me. But what about your family?"

"They're well provided for. And, anyway, Karl would have wanted you to have it."

"Then, I accept your generous gift. I can't remember the last time we had fresh meat."

"And I thank you again, Dieter," Ernst said. "When do you return to duty?"

"I catch the early morning train the day after tomorrow."

"Then you and Lili should go and have a good time. Don't worry about me. I'll be fine."

He offered his hand, which Dieter gripped firmly.

"Good luck, Ernst."

"My war is over, Dieter. It's you who'll need the good luck."

Chapter 6

SOLDIERS HOME ON LEAVE WERE IGNORED ON THE streets of Freiburg. In the early years of the war, men in uniform would have been greeted with smiles and handshakes from complete strangers wishing them well. Now they just reminded civilians of a war that had gone on too long.

Along Kaiser Joseph Strasse, Dieter and Lili passed several long lines of people waiting patiently outside shops to purchase whatever rationed necessities of life happened to be in stock that day. Dieter wondered if Lili would bring up again the subject of the black market. Like many Germans, he had no qualms about breaking the ration laws if it helped to make life a little bit easier in these difficult times. Obviously, Lili felt differently. Dieter reached into one of his coat pockets and touched a piece of Dutch chocolate he'd purchased for Lili from a grocer who dealt illegally in the black market. It was better left in his pocket, he concluded. He wasn't one to go looking for an argument.

As they entered the cathedral square, the Hosanna rang out the noon Angelus. Across the square, in front of the cathedral, passersby stopped and gathered before the rector, Father Keidel, for the mid-day devotion. Dieter and Lili decided to join in. At the conclusion of the prayer, Dieter turned to Lili.

"How about a glass of wine?" he asked.

Lili took his arm. "I'd like that very much," she replied with a smile.

As they turned towards a nearby café, a voice called out Dieter's name. They turned to see Father Keidel coming towards them. Dieter walked towards the elderly priest, but Lili held back.

"How is your father, Dieter?" Father Keidel asked as he drew closer.

Dieter's father had taken Karl's death hard. An eventual breakdown had forced Professor Hannsen to take a leave of absence from his teaching duties at the university. Since his release from the hospital, his father spent his days in his study staring out the window. "There's not much change, I'm afraid, Father."

"I'm sorry to hear that, Dieter. I will continue to pray for his recovery."

"My aunt and I are grateful for your prayers." His father's youngest sister, Ingrid, had come with her two children, Tomas and Anna, from Hamburg in northern Germany to look after him. Ingrid's husband had been killed in the first month of the war.

The priest looked over Dieter's shoulder. "I see that Lili Bloch is with you."

"*Ja.*"

"I would like a few words with her, if you don't mind. I won't be a minute."

"Of course."

Respecting the priest's request for a moment of privacy, Dieter moved off in the opposite direction. Nearby, six prisoners of war swept the square under the supervision of two policemen. Dieter's attention was drawn to one of the prisoners who was taller than the others. This prisoner stood out in another way. Unlike the other five, who were dressed in drab civilian clothing, he still wore his uniform. The others, Dieter concluded, had been prisoners for some time; the tall one, on the other hand, had been captured fairly recently. Red stripes had been painted down his trousers and on the sleeves and back of his tunic. He wouldn't get far if he tried to escape.

The tall prisoner returned Dieter's stare with a look

of defiance. Then one of the policemen shouted at him to get back to work. In the next moment Lili was by his side. "Shall we go?" she asked. As they walked to the café, Dieter couldn't resist one more look in the direction of the prisoners. The tall one was back pushing his broom.

A glass of Freiburg's wine was one of the few pleasures in life the war hadn't stolen. By the time the waiter poured their second glasses, the conversation had turned to the prisoners in the square.

"I couldn't help but notice," Lili was saying, "the exchange of cold stares between you and the tall prisoner."

"I was more curious than anything. Did you notice the maple leaf buttons on the collar of his tunic?" Dieter was surprised that some German soldier hadn't taken the buttons as souvenirs. "He's a Canadian."

"I've read in the newspaper," Lili said, "that Canadian soldiers should be despised as mercenaries."

Dieter gave a shrug. "Many Canadians were born in Britain or still have family there. I guess their loyalty to their mother country is still strong."

"You seem to know something about Canada."

"My father took Karl and me there the winter before the war started to visit his brother. One day I did something very foolish which could've cost me my life. If a Canadian hadn't come to my rescue, I wouldn't be here now enjoying your company."

"Then you must feel some compassion for this Canadian prisoner."

"I suppose I do."

Lili paused to glance out a nearby window that overlooked the square. When she looked at him again, Dieter expected to see anger in her face. Instead, there was only sorrow. "I wish, Dieter, I could say the same. Ever since my parents were killed, I've been consumed by hate. I've prayed that the French airmen who murdered them would burn in hell."

"That's understandable, Lili. Your parents were innocent civilians."

"Yes, Dieter, but not acceptable, not in God's eyes. I've been living a life unworthy of a Christian. Jesus taught us to love and forgive our enemies. Lately, I haven't been taking communion. That's why Father Keidel wanted to speak to me in the square."

Dieter paused to take a sip of wine and reflect on Lili's words. "You remind me of Karl. He always wanted to do the right thing."

"And you, Dieter, you don't feel compelled to do the right thing?"

"I usually start out with the best intentions, but more often than not I end up taking the path of least resistance."

"I doubt that very much. This morning you came to my rescue."

Dieter wondered what Lili would say if she knew the whole story, that he'd let the thief go. "You don't really know me."

"I remember you that night at the recital. I thought you looked so handsome."

"It must have been Karl you remember."

"*Nein*, it was definitely you." The angelic smile had returned. "You seemed so uncomfortable, dressed up for this formal event, as if you wanted to be somewhere else."

"I prefer the outdoors. Hunting, fishing, hiking, sailing…" Dieter stopped, suddenly aware that something was wrong. The conversations at nearby tables had become louder and more animated. Many of the patrons were staring out the window of the café. Dieter looked to see the cause of the commotion. In the square, a short distance away, about a dozen middle-aged men had gathered. Even through the café windows Dieter could hear their shouts of anger. In their midst he could see the tall prisoner. The Canadian was in trouble.

The look of defiance had gone. The Canadian was now afraid, and with good reason. By the time Dieter and Lili arrived, the mood of the men had turned ugly. Dieter recognized some of them. They were among the town's prominent citizens. The other prisoners, he noted, huddled together off to one side, thankful that they weren't involved, but well aware they could be next.

"Why do you fight in a war that has nothing to do with you?" asked the man who was standing in front of Dieter and Lili. It was Herr Leidenberger, a merchant.

It was clear from the puzzled look on his face that the Canadian didn't understand German. Did he comprehend, Dieter wondered, why the crowd was so angry with him?

"He's nothing but a hired killer!" shouted another man whom Dieter didn't know. Next to him, dressed in his bowler hat and carrying his ivory-handled walking stick, was Herr Strasser, the banker, a menacing look covering his face like a dark cloud. Herr Strasser, Dieter remembered, had lost two sons to the war.

Herr Leidenburger wasn't finished. "The newspapers say Canadians don't take prisoners. Well, the people of Freiburg don't take prisoners!"

The crowd, now grown larger, roared its agreement.

Dieter looked at the policemen, standing to one side, their arms folded, smiling grimly. This could get out of hand, he thought, but he was reluctant to get involved. He turned to Lili, taking her arm. "It's best we leave."

"No," she answered. Pulling her arm away, she pushed past Herr Leidenberger. "Let me through!" she shouted. "Let me through!"

At that same moment, Herr Strasser lunged forward and struck the prisoner over the head with his walking stick. The Canadian crumpled to his knees, blood running down his face. As the banker raised his stick to strike again, Lili stepped in front of him, using her tiny body to shield the injured prisoner. "Stop it!" she cried out. "How can you attack a defenceless man?"

A hush fell over the crowd.

"Step aside, girl," someone called out. "This is a man's business. Go home where you belong."

Seizing the opportunity, Dieter moved quickly to grab hold of Herr Strasser's arm to prevent a further blow. Tears in the banker's eyes were trickling down his cheeks into his grey beard. "Sir," Dieter said gently, "he's just a poor soldier who's done his duty. Leave him in peace."

Herr Strasser nodded and let his arm go limp. The two policemen, now shamed into doing their duty, moved in and dispersed the crowd. Two of the prisoners rushed over to help their injured comrade. One of them, in heavily accented German, said to Lili, "*Danke, Fraulein.*"

Soon Dieter and Lili stood alone, in silence. Dieter wasn't sure what to say. Of one thing he was certain: he felt deeply ashamed. Herr Strasser may well have killed the prisoner had Lili not intervened. She'd found the courage to do what was right. And he hadn't. God had given him a chance to repay a debt, and he had failed to act.

It was Lili who spoke first. "I interpret your silence, Dieter, to mean that you agree with what that man said, that I had no business interfering, that I should have kept my place."

Before he had a chance to reply, she turned and walked away.

Chapter 7

THE TRAIN RIDE TO THE TITISEE TOOK ABOUT AN HOUR. As a youth, Dieter had often visited this glacial lake in the mountains to the east of Freiburg. In the lake, and the surrounding forest, he'd found a refuge from the pressures of daily life. Now, after the incident in the cathedral square, he needed a place to sort things out.

At the Titisee, he set out on a hiking trail that followed the shoreline. The air was cold but not enough to freeze the lake whose waves lapped against the nearby shore. Dieter thought of the Canadian prisoner, so far away from his home, a country where the winters were more severe than here in the Black Forest.

Their father had taken Dieter and Karl to Canada to visit his brother for the Christmas holiday of 1913. Their uncle lived in Ottawa where he'd become a successful fur merchant since emigrating to Canada before Dieter was born.

They sailed to New York and then took the train to the Canadian capital. The boys looked forward to skiing and tobogganing, but there had been little snow in Ottawa that December. An early cold snap, however, permitted the opening of the city's skating rinks. The boys had learned to skate years earlier while visiting their mother's family in Holland.

The highlight of their visit was an invitation to a pre-Christmas skating party at Rideau Hall, the residence of the Governor-General of Canada. The Governor-General at the time was the Duke of Connaught. The Duke's wife was a German princess. At the party, the professor and his sons were introduced to the Duke and Duchess and their daughter, Princess Patricia.

The rink at Rideau Hall overlooked the Ottawa River. Guests were warned not to skate on the river. A tragic accident had occurred around the turn of the century. A young woman had gone through the ice while skating on the river and a young man had jumped into save her. Both had drowned.

It wasn't long before Dieter got bored on the crowded, confined rink. While his father and uncle were busy talking with the viceregal couple and Karl was skating with Princess Patricia, he slipped away unnoticed and went down to the river. On a boat dock he laced on his skates and stepped out onto the ice. It seemed solid. To his left, about a half kilometre away, a man skated near the shore, cradling a puck in the blade of a hockey stick. He appeared to be practising left and right turns. Dieter figured the fellow wouldn't be out on the ice if it weren't safe.

After a while, Dieter decided to venture farther out. Looking to the opposite shore, he saw the mouth of another river that emptied into the Ottawa. That should have been a warning to stop. The fast-flowing current of one river combining with another would have kept the surface at that point from freezing. Dieter would have seen the open water had it not been growing dark. He could hear it. But it was too late.

At first he was surprised that the water didn't feel colder than it did. Then he realized that the water was actually a few degrees warmer than the air. He was a strong swimmer and confident he could swim to where the ice was firm and pull himself out. But the weight of his waterlogged clothing and the pull of the strong current made it difficult. He started to panic.

Then a voice called out to him to hold on. In the twilight, he could make out a figure crawling on the ice towards him, reaching out to him with a hockey stick.

With one last desperate effort Dieter swam towards the stick and grabbed on.

His rescuer was a professional hockey player named Liam Cassidy. That day Liam had been taking advantage of the early freeze-up to enjoy a skate on the river. He knew enough, however, to stay close to the shore. When he saw Dieter head out towards the opposite shore, he immediately set out after him, arriving just in time to pull him out of the water.

Liam had come to see the young teenager in the hospital the next day and invited him to an upcoming hockey game at the city's arena. It was Liam's first season as a professional and his team, the Ottawa Senators, were playing the Montreal Canadiens. Dieter thoroughly enjoyed himself, fascinated by the speed of the game, although Liam had been injured when he was cut over the eye by the stick of an opposing player.

The next day Dieter had visited Liam at his home, a row house where he lived with his mother and his sister. On the wall in the kitchen was mounted a rifle. Liam, it turned out, shared Dieter's passion for hunting. The rifle, the American army Springfield Model 1903, was Liam's pride and joy. He'd had it modified by a local gunsmith for hunting. Dieter had read about the American rifle that employed the German Mauser bolt action, and he leapt at Liam's offer to try it out. The two ended up spending hours together roaming the woods near the city hunting deer. Dieter had finally found a friend who shared his love for the outdoors.

By the end of Dieter's visit, early in the new year, they'd become good friends. They parted at Ottawa's Union Station with a promise from Dieter to visit again. It was a promise never kept. The war had seen to that.

✦

Dieter watched a stag stop for a drink on the opposite shore of the Titisee before bounding off into the forest. An animal's existence, he mused, was so straightforward. Life for humans, on the other hand, was infinitely more complex. There were always choices to make, and rarely were any of them easy. This morning in the square he'd made the wrong choice, and now he had to make his peace with God.

He looked at his wristwatch. If he hurried, he could get back to Freiburg in time.

It was late afternoon when Dieter entered the cathedral. He was relieved to find that Father Keidel was still hearing confessions. He entered the confessional and knelt. On the other side of the partition the priest slid open the panel that allowed him to hear what Dieter had to say.

"Bless me, Father," Dieter began, "for I have sinned. Four years ago a man risked his life to save mine. This morning in the square I had the chance to repay him by coming to the aid of a countryman of his. Instead, I stood by and did nothing. Had it not been for Lili Bloch, this man would most likely have been killed."

There was a pause before the priest spoke. "Some parishioners told me about the incident in the square, Dieter. Lili Bloch acted with great courage, did she not?'

"Of course, Father. She was very brave."

"Do you think Lili was motivated by a desire to repay a debt?"

Dieter stopped to think before answering. "No, Father, I don't suppose she was. She was simply coming to the aid of an unarmed man. I guess you could say Lili was obeying her conscience."

"It is something that God expects of all of us, Dieter. You disappointed Him, not by failing to repay a friend, but by turning your back on a fellow human being."

"I understand now, Father."

"Then I absolve you from all of your sins. In the name of the Father, the Son and the Holy Ghost. Go in peace."

Chapter 8

February 12, 1918

LIAM HAILED A TAXI IN FRONT OF THE VICTORIA LEAGUE Club on Charing Cross Road in London's West End and climbed into the back seat.

"Where to, guv?" the driver asked.

"The Empire on Park Lane."

The driver turned around. "Are you sure?"

Liam noticed the perplexed look on his face but thought nothing of it. "Yeah, I'm sure."

"Right-o," the driver said as he pulled away from the curb.

The streets of London were congested with late afternoon traffic, and it wasn't long before the taxi came to a halt. Liam stared out the window in wonder at the crowds of people who were enjoying the sudden improvement in the weather. The clear sky and pleasant temperature were unusual for southern England in February.

The driver looked back over his shoulder, a knowing look on his face. "A lot bigger than 'ome, I wager." Liam nodded his head, while switching his gaze to the other window. The traffic started to move again, and the taxi lurched forward.

The driver continued to talk and negotiate the traffic at the same time. "How're the accommodations at the Victoria League Club?"

The place where Liam was staying was one of two

in London set up by the British King and Queen to give overseas soldiers a comfortable, but inexpensive, place to stay while on leave. "I'd forgotten what it's like to sleep in a real bed," Liam answered. "And the food's good."

Liam might have mentioned the telephones as well, one of which he'd used to contact Rose at the Empire half an hour earlier. His original plan had been to try to reach her that morning after breakfast. However, he'd talked himself out of it. She'd probably made other plans. Or, more likely, she'd forgotten all about him.

So Liam had spent the day taking in the sights of London, trying to have a good time. But he couldn't get Rose out of his mind. As he wandered the streets he found himself whistling the tune of "Roses of Picardy", a popular wartime song.

Roses are shining in Picardy
In the hush of the silver dew.
Roses are flowering in Picardy
But there's never a rose like you.

The lyrics spoke for Liam's heart.

By mid-afternoon he'd worked up enough courage to telephone her. Rose had sounded glad to hear from him. "I was so afraid, Liam, that you'd forgotten me," she said. "Yes, of course, I would be happy to have dinner with you this evening. I'll meet you in the hotel lobby at six."

Now, as he sat in the back of a taxi making its way through the streets of London, Liam was kicking himself for not having phoned sooner.

The driver continued the conversation. "They say the American YMCA's more expensive, but they sell real ice cream."

Liam was starting to get used to his heavy cockney accent. "I haven't had ice cream since I left Ottawa."

"I've had many Canucks in me cab. And Aussies, Frenchies, Yanks, you name it. Now those Yanks, they take the cake. Bold as brass, that lot. Think they're goin' to win the bleedin' war for us."

Just then the traffic ground to another halt. Liam glanced out the window on his left. A tattered poster stuck to the wall of a nearby building caught his eye. It depicted a German soldier as a bloodthirsty ape, drooling over the body of a woman.

The driver turned to say something and followed Liam's stare to the poster. "Huns." He spat out the word. "The bloody animals killed Billy at the Somme. Me only son, God bless 'is soul."

"I'm sorry." Liam couldn't think of anything else to say.

"Never knew a German I liked," the driver continued.

Liam thought of Dieter Hannsen. "I knew one once," he said. He seemed okay to me, he was about to add, but changed his mind.

The traffic started up again.

"They're all the same," the driver snapped as he pulled out to pass a horse-drawn cart. "Treacherous lot." He muttered something else, which Liam didn't catch, and then fell silent.

Liam was thankful for the silence. He was trying to put the war out of his mind, and the conversation hadn't helped much. It was Rose he wanted to think about. Who was this American girl who had the pluck to drive an ambulance in wartime and yet was so afraid of submarines? He wanted to know more about her, so much more.

The driver made a turn onto a street lined on the left with the grand homes of the rich. "Park Lane," he announced to Liam. "That's 'yde Park on your right." Liam turned his head to see an elegantly dressed couple horseback riding through the park.

"And this," the driver said as he pulled over to the curb, "is the Empire."

Liam looked back to his left out the window. "This is it?" he asked, astounded.

"The Empire in all its glory, mate. Definitely one of London's finer 'otels. Where them 'igh mucky-mucks stay when they visit London."

Rose could afford to stay in a fancy place like this? Liam started to wonder what he had got himself into.

Just then another taxi pulled up behind. A British major got out and headed for the hotel entrance. " 'E's what I usually bring to the Empire," the driver said. "Never an enlisted bloke like yourself."

Liam got out of the taxi, paid his fare, and said, "Thanks."

"Do me a favour, will you, lad?"

"Sure," Liam answered.

"The next time you have a Hun in your sights, say to yourself, 'This one's for Billy, Lester Braddock's son,' and then blow 'is brains out. Will you do that for me, mate?"

"Yeah, sure," Liam answered.

The driver gave him a wave and drove off. Watching him disappear into the traffic, Liam wondered if Lester asked all his soldier passengers the same favour.

The doorman outside the Empire gave Liam an icy stare. His unspoken message was clear: common soldiers are not welcome here, so move along. Liam turned and faced the street, his fists clenched at his side, anger churning his stomach. He didn't know whether he was angrier with the doorman for looking down his nose at him or with Rose for suggesting they meet in the hotel.

A memory came rushing back of the day he'd tried as a boy to enter the main lobby of the Russell House to give his mother a message. The doorman had grabbed him by the collar of his coat and led him unceremoniously to the sidewalk.

"But me mother works here," young Liam had protested, his eyes filling with tears.

"Scullery maids use the rear door," the doorman growled. "Now be off with you, or you'll feel the back of my hand."

The humiliation of that day still stung. And it's not, Liam decided, about to be repeated now. Turning to face the Empire's doorman, Liam was startled to see him coming towards him. His eyes, however, were looking past Liam. As the doorman brushed by, Liam glanced over his shoulder to see a taxi parked at the curb. In the back seat was a British colonel. As the doorman reached to open the taxi door, Liam seized the opportunity, sprinted up the steps, pushed through the revolving doors and entered the Empire.

So far, so good, he thought to himself. That was easier than I thought it was going to be.

Inside, he quickly took in the layout of the lobby. To his left was the main desk. Behind it stood a man with his back to him, tending to some business. In the middle of the lobby was a grand, elaborately carved wooden staircase leading to the second floor. To the right of the staircase, against the back wall, Liam could see the door to the lift. Next to it was a floor clock. The time was five minutes past six. Apart from the man behind the desk, the lobby was empty. Everyone, Liam concluded, must be in the dining room. But there was no sign of Rose. Liam started to panic. Where could she be?

He considered asking the man behind the desk but then thought better of it. A glance over his shoulder told him he'd better do something quick. About to enter through the revolving doors was the British colonel. Behind him was the doorman, loaded down with parcels. Looking to his right, Liam saw a doorway. An escape route — or a trap? He'd have to take his chances.

He darted through the doorway to find himself in an elegantly decorated and finely furnished sitting room. Seated opposite the doorway near a fireplace was an elderly man reading a newspaper. On seeing Liam, the man dropped his newspaper, the look of bewilderment on his face quickly turning to a frown. Ja-sus, Liam thought, I'm done for now. "Pardon me, sir," he stammered. "I was just — "

"Liam."

Someone had spoken his name. It was Rose! Liam turned his head in the direction of her voice. There she was on a settee near a window. Seated next to her was a girl. Rose stood up and came towards him, glancing at the clock on the mantle of the fireplace. "I'm terribly sorry, Liam. I lost track of the time."

The very sight of Rose made Liam forget for a moment his predicament. Her smile was even more beautiful than he'd remembered.

The elderly man got up from his chair and passed behind Rose, muttering to himself as he headed towards the lobby. However, Liam took no notice of him. He couldn't take his eyes off Rose. "This is a little fancier than our first meetin' place," he said. Then, remembering the colonel, he added, "But maybe we should be on our way."

"Yes, of course, Liam. But first I would like someone to meet you." She took him by the arm and led him towards the girl on the settee. She was about sixteen years old. There was sadness in her eyes, Liam noted, that her smile failed to hide.

"Meredith, I would like you to meet Liam Cassidy, the soldier I've been telling you about. Liam, this is Meredith Fotherby."

"How do you do," Meredith said as she stood up and extended her hand.

Shaking it, Liam said, "Pleased to meet you, miss."

"No, Private Cassidy, the pleasure is mine. We are very grateful to the people of Canada for the help they have so generously given to the mother country."

If you only knew the truth about me, Liam thought. "We're happy to do our part," he managed to say without feeling too guilty. She didn't need to know that he had been a reluctant volunteer.

"Please accept my congratulations for your great victory at Vimy Ridge." The previous April, forty thousand soldiers of the Canadian Corps had succeeded in dislodging the Germans from a major stronghold near the French village of Vimy.

"Thanks," Liam said. "Actually, I wasn't there," he went on to explain. "I'm with the Canadian Cavalry Brigade. We're attached to the British Fifth Army."

"Meredith's from Liverpool," Rose said. "She's travelled to London to be with her father while he's on leave."

"My father's a colonel in the army," Meredith added. "We've taken rooms here at the Empire."

A British colonel. The panic returned. "And where's your father now?" Liam asked.

"On a shopping excursion, purchasing clothing and toiletries that will make life at the front more bearable. Father says conditions in the trenches are ghastly."

I don't recall seeing too many colonels in the trenches, Liam was about to say, but bit his tongue. "I sure can vouch for that," he said instead. The colonel, Liam figured, must have gone to his room. Before long he would return to the lobby looking for his daughter. If he found her with Liam, an enlisted man from the colonies, there would be hell to pay.

"I offered to spend the afternoon with Meredith," Rose explained. "We went out for lunch and then explored the city before returning to the hotel for tea. Just in time, I might add, for your telephone call."

"That sounds very nice." Liam tried not to sound impatient, but the look of annoyance on Rose's face told him he wasn't succeeding.

"Liam, you're behaving very —"

A booming, male voice prevented Rose from finishing her sentence. "I demand to know the meaning of this!"

Liam knew immediately he was in trouble. Big trouble. As he turned around, Liam found himself face to face with the British colonel who had followed him into the hotel. The colonel was livid. Standing behind him was the doorman, with an equally menacing look on his face. Liam immediately drew himself to attention and saluted smartly.

"Father," he heard Meredith say, her voice cracking.

Rose, however, spoke with no trace of fear. "Colonel Fotherby, how good to see you. I hope your shopping trip went well."

The colonel simply ignored Rose and continued to glower at Liam. "How dare you set foot in this hotel and speak with my daughter. I have a good mind to call the military police. A night in the guardhouse will teach you to know your place." The colonel's words dripped with contempt. It took all of Liam's self-control to remain at attention, his eyes straight ahead.

"Please, Father, this man has caused me no

harm." Meredith's plea earned her a stern look from the colonel, and she said no more.

Rose was not so easily intimidated. "This soldier's here at my invitation, Colonel Fotherby."

"Then you should have known better, Miss Pearce. The Empire's clientele is restricted to officers and people of social rank. The hotel's guests are deeply offended by the presence of this common soldier, especially one from the colonies."

"Colonel, really — "

"I will discuss the matter with you no more, Miss Pearce," the colonel interrupted. "As for you, Private, you can consider yourself lucky that I have decided not to place you under arrest. Now get out of my sight!"

"Yes, sir." Liam saluted again and then quickly left the sitting room with the doorman right behind him.

In the lobby, the doorman caught up to him and took hold of his arm. "It'll be my pleasure to show an ill-mannered colonial to the sidewalk," he snarled.

With his free hand, Liam reached across and grabbed the man's wrist in vice-like grip and squeezed until the man let go of his arm with a cry of pain. "I know the way out," Liam said. The doorman backed away, rubbing his bruised wrist.

At that moment the sound of raised voices carried into the lobby from the sitting room. Both men stopped to listen. "You should be ashamed of yourself, Colonel Fotherby!" There was no mistaking Rose's voice.

"How dare you speak to me that way, Miss Pearce!"

"Let me see if I understand you correctly, Colonel. That soldier is good enough to risk life and limb for the glorious British Empire, but he's not good enough to set foot in one of your grand hotels."

"Your opinion, Miss Pearce, is of no importance to me."

"My opinion, Colonel, is that this war will have served no purpose unless it rids the world of your medieval obsession with social class."

The angry exchange of words left the doorman looking absolutely mortified. "Americans," he said. "Such an ill-mannered people. I wish we didn't have to rely on their help to win the war."

"I know how you feel, chum," Liam said as he headed for the revolving doors. "I wish I didn't need her help to fight my personal battles, either."

Outside on the sidewalk, Liam hailed a taxi parked across the street next to the park. The driver started the engine and, making a U-turn, pulled up in front of the Empire. As he opened the rear door to get in, he heard Rose call out to him, "Liam, please wait."

Liam stopped, hesitated, and then said to the driver, "Give me a minute, will you."

The driver nodded. Liam turned and looked at Rose, her face still flushed from her confrontation with the Colonel.

"I'm truly sorry, Liam. I should have known something like this would happen. I should have suggested we meet elsewhere."

"Why?"

"Why? Because the British are the world's worst snobs."

"I'm not talking about that brass hat in the hotel. I have to put up with his kind every day. Most Canadian officers are no better. I mean, why me? Why would a woman like you, who can afford to stay in a place like this, care for someone the likes of me? Is this some kind of game you're playin'? A bit of slummin' to see how the other half lives?"

He could see that he'd hurt her.

"You don't understand, Liam."

"Hey, guv." It was the driver. "I've got a livin' to make."

Liam answered him without taking his eyes off Rose. "Do you know a good Irish pub?"

"Sure. There's one not far from here. Jump in."

Liam extended his hand towards Rose, inviting her to join him in the back seat.

"Maybe you can help me understand."

Chapter 9

THE SIGN ABOVE THE DOOR READ "MICKEY O'Rourke's". The man who showed Liam and Rose to a table was of a stout, but sturdy, build, with his sleeves rolled up and an apron tied around his waist. He introduced himself as the owner.

Mickey O'Rourke had the look of man who was indifferent to the problems of the world, but when he heard Liam speak, his eyes brightened. "A transplanted Irishman," he exclaimed.

"Second generation," Liam answered. "Mum and Dad came from the old country."

"Well, boy-o," Mickey said, "you should've stayed in Canada. The only thing waitin' for you in France is a German bullet."

"It's a long story."

Mickey gave a shrug and dropped the subject. "I haven't much to eat. Just a bit of fish and sausage. No chips. Food shortage, you know."

"Whatever you have will be fine," Rose said with a smile. Mickey nodded and ambled off to the kitchen behind the bar.

At first they ate their food in silence, neither sure of what to say. Rose was the first to speak. "We shouldn't be too hard on Colonel Fotherby. He's suffered a great deal."

Liam finished a mouthful of fish. "It's nothin' to bother yourself about. He means nothin' to me."

But Rose persisted. "Both his sons were killed in France. Their loss was too much for his wife who was already in poor health. She passed away last October. Meredith is all he has left."

Liam thought for a moment before speaking. "That explains why she looks older than her years."

"I intend to apologize to both of them for my behaviour when I return to the hotel."

"Suit yourself." Liam finished another mouthful of fish. "Anyway, I'm the one who should be apologizin'. I'm sure this fish doesn't measure up to the food they serve at the Empire."

"It's fine, thank you," Rose answered with a smile. "Far better than what we get at the hospital in France."

Liam put down his cutlery and looked at her face. Her eyes were a vivid blue and there was a hint of colour in her cheeks. "Rose, you have the most beautiful smile I've ever seen."

The colour in Rose's cheeks darkened. "Well, aren't you the forward one, Liam Cassidy!"

Liam wondered if he had gone too far. "I'm sorry if I spoke out of turn. It's just that ... I've been wantin' to tell you since we met on the ferry."

Rose laughed. "I'm just teasing, Liam. I am flattered. Thank you for the compliment. Now it's my turn," she continued. "There's something about your face that intrigues me."

"You mean the scar."

"Yes. Is it from a war injury?

"Nah," Liam laughed. "Just somethin' I picked up in a hockey game."

"You mean ice hockey."

Liam nodded.

"Such a violent game, ice hockey," she continued after a pause.

"It has its moments."

"That surprises me, Liam."

"Why's that?"

"You don't strike me as being a particularly violent man. And yet you play a violent sport."

Liam smiled. "I thought we came here to learn more about you."

"In good time."

"Yeah, well, I like the game. And it provides a decent pay cheque."

"You're a professional?"

"I play for the Ottawa Senators. In the off-season I work in a lumberyard. There's enough to pay the bills and look after me mum."

"That's very thoughtful of you, Liam, to take care of your mother."

"It's the least I can do. After me dad died, she worked hard to provide for me and my sister."

"How did your father die?"

"He was killed in a fire, trying to save the horses at the sawmill where he worked. The fire ended up destroyin' the part of the city where we lived."

"That must've been terrible, Liam. I'm so sorry. I can understand the pain you must have felt. I lost both my parents when I was six years old."

Liam was taken aback. "Me mum always said there's always someone worse off than yourself. What happened, Rose?"

"There was a terrible storm in '98, the worst in living memory. They were taking a steamer home from Boston for Thanksgiving. They never made it. Everyone on board was lost."

"That must have been a terrible blow for a

young girl."

"I was fortunate to have a kind and loving grandfather who took me in and raised me. He was a sea captain. He sailed the oceans of the world in his clipper ship until the steam engine forced him into retirement."

Liam thought about of the luxury of the Empire. "There must have been a dollar or two to be made sailin' the seas."

Rose smiled. "He did all right for himself. Certainly well enough to put his granddaughter up in an expensive hotel."

Just then Mickey returned with a bottle of Irish whiskey and a glass. "On the house," he said. "From one Irishman to another."

"Thanks anyway," Liam said, "but I'll pass tonight."

"What, an Irishman who doesn't enjoy his whiskey!" Mickey said, a puzzled look on his face.

"I'm not Irish. I'm a Canadian," Liam said, unable to hide the edge in his voice.

"Suit yourself."

"And what about me?" Rose said to Mickey.

"Now there's a lass after me own heart." Mickey filled the glass, set it down in front of Rose and returned to the bar.

Watching Rose take a sip, Liam could tell it wasn't the first time whiskey had passed her lips. "Where I come from ladies don't drink that stuff."

Rose laughed. "That was Granddad's one regret. That he didn't raise me to be the lady his daughter would have wanted me to become."

"Tell me more about your grandfather."

"He's a man who fears nothing, not even the fury of the sea. I think I became the son he always wanted. He taught me to swim, to sail, to use a sextant. He was the first man in Barnstable to own an automobile which he taught me to drive."

Rose took another swallow of whiskey. "And on my eighteenth birthday he introduced me to the nectar of the Emerald Isle. Are you sure you won't join me?"

If you only knew how hard it is for me to say no, Liam wanted to say. "Maybe later. You speak of your grandfather with great affection."

"He's the only man I've ever known who treated me like a human being with enough intelligence to make my own decisions in life."

"So you decided to go to war."

"I wanted to do my part."

"And your grandfather approved?"

"A week after I told him of my decision, he booked passage for me on … on the *Lusitania*."

Liam shook his head in astonishment. Rose was certainly one for surprises. "You mean to tell me, Rose … ?"

She nodded. "Yes, Liam, I was on board the *Lusitania* when she was torpedoed."

Liam remembered how frightened Rose had looked that day on the ferry out of Boulogne. "No wonder," he said, "you're afraid of submarines."

The colour in Rose's cheeks was suddenly gone and, when she spoke, there was a cold hardness in her voice. "Until that day I had never understood what it meant to hate. Now I despise the German people with every fibre in my body. They deserve to be condemned as the Hun of modern history."

First, Lester Braddock, Liam thought, and now Rose — two people who had good reason to hate Germans. Once again it seemed like the wrong time to mention Dieter Hannsen. Better, he figured, to change the subject. "I don't suppose you'd be interested in seein' some of London with me tomorrow?"

The suggestion brought a smile back to Rose's face.

"There's nothing I would like better, Liam."

"I'm glad to hear you say that, Rose."

After they finished their meal, they caught a taxi, which dropped Rose at the Empire before taking Liam to the Victoria League Club where he settled in for the night. Unable to sleep, Liam kept going over the day's events in his mind.

Rose was like no other woman he'd ever met. The girls of Le Breton Flats tended to be mild mannered, even mousy, in some cases. Even the bolder ones knew there was a line they couldn't cross. Women where Liam came from knew their place. Rose, however, seemed to put no limits on herself. She had a mind of her own and a will to use it, regardless of what anyone else thought. Liam could see how her strong sense of independence might drive some men away. Was he one of those men? He wasn't sure. All he knew was that he longed to see her again.

Finally, his thoughts turned to Dieter Hannsen. Memories of Dieter surfaced from time to time, often unexpectedly. It was something that his German friend had said once that Liam now remembered. They'd been hunting one day in the hills on the Quebec side of the Ottawa River. Dieter had just brought down a large buck with Liam's Springfield. As they stood over the dead animal, he asked Liam if he minded a personal question.

"No," Liam had replied, "what's on your mind?"

Dieter looked him in the eye. "Could you ever kill a man?"

"Ja-sus, Dieter, what kind of question is that!"

"I mean in war, Liam. Could you ever kill a man in battle?"

Liam considered the question before answering. "It's somethin' I've never thought about. My country doesn't have any enemies."

Dieter surveyed the surrounding hills, their trees shrouded in freshly fallen snow. "Your country is very beautiful." Then he looked at Liam once more. There was a sadness in his eyes. "Germany's not so fortunate. France and Russia are allied against us. One day we must fight them."

Seven months later Germany was at war. Its enemies now included Canada. But, unlike Lester Braddock and Rose Pearce, Liam had no reason to hate Germans. They weren't his enemy. One of them was his friend.

Eventually sleep came, but not the dreamless slumber Liam yearned for. The dream had been recurring each night since his arrival in London. It was always the same — a small group of soldiers, with sombre expressions, gathered around another who cradled a boot in his hands.

The man holding the boot was John Latimer.

The boot was Liam's.

Chapter 10

February 12, 1918

IT WAS THE FINAL DAY OF HIS LEAVE, AND DIETER Hannsen was determined to make the most of it.

Through the frosted panes of his bedroom window he could make out wisps of cirrus clouds high in the sky, greeting the early morning sun with the promise of a perfect day for hiking in the forest. The evening would be spent with his aunt and his two cousins. Maybe even his father might join them at the dinner table. But first he should attend mass.

By the time he reached the Schwabentor, the Angelus was ringing in the cathedral's tower. He found a seat near the rear the cathedral and knelt to pray. Shortly afterwards Father Keidel, accompanied by two altar boys, appeared at the altar to celebrate the mass. Off to his left, a few rows ahead of him, Dieter recognized a woman's hat. It belonged to Lili Bloch. They hadn't spoken since the incident in the square the previous morning. When it came time to receive communion, Dieter rose with the rest of the worshippers and moved to the railing in front of the altar. Lili, he noted, joined them. It appeared that she'd found the inner peace she was looking for. Dieter was glad for her.

At the conclusion of the mass, Dieter sought out Father Keidel to say goodbye and then headed for the main doors. There waiting for him was Lili, looking anxious. "Dieter, I thought I might have missed you. Do you have a moment?"

"Of course," Dieter, replied, unsure of what to expect. He was still smarting from the sting of Lili's tongue.

"Dieter, I want to apologize for my rudeness yesterday. What I said was uncalled for. I'm afraid I have this habit sometimes of speaking without thinking first. I hope you'll forgive me."

"An apology isn't necessary, Lili. You put all those men, including me, to shame. Your courage saved a man's life."

"You would've done the same, Dieter. I've no doubt of that."

"Well, I'd like to think so."

Lili placed a hand on his arm and, standing on her toes, kissed him softly on the cheek. "*Auf Wiedersehen*, Dieter," she whispered. "God be with you."

As she turned to walk away, Dieter hesitated, knowing what he wanted to say, but unsure of how to say it. "Wait, Lili," he stammered. "We don't have to say goodbye, do we, at least not yet?"

Lili stopped and looked back in expectation.

"I guess what I'm trying to say is … would you spend the day with me?"

Lili broke into a smile. "I was hoping you would ask."

As Dieter returned the smile, a slight gasp of relief escaped his lips. "How about a walk in the forest?" he asked.

"But, Dieter, it's so cold."

"Come with me to my house and I'll find something warmer for you to wear."

She laughed. "All right then."

It occurred to Dieter that the day was turning out to be even better than he hoped for.

The topic of discussion that evening at the Hannsen dinner table was Dieter's venison, which made the old potatoes and unappetizing war bread his aunt served with it at least tolerable. "That was heavenly, Frau Kaufmann," Lili said as she finished her meal. "I was very hungry after our hike in the forest."

"I'm just pleased that Dieter invited you to dinner, Lili. It's not often we have company any more. I'm just sorry the professor is not able to join us."

"Lili," Dieter interjected, "why don't you have this last portion of meat." He picked up the platter in one hand and the server in the other.

"*Nein*, Dieter, *danke*," she protested. "It would be wrong of me to have more than my share. The children should come first."

"I won't accept no for an answer," Dieter replied as he placed the piece of roasted venison on Lili's plate. "Don't worry about these two," he continued, grinning at his two cousins, seated side by side across the table. "They're saving room for their chocolate treat."

"We can't wait!" Anna exclaimed.

"Anna!" Ingrid scolded. "Don't be bold!"

"*Ja, Mutti*," the eight-year-old replied, the expression of glee gone as quickly it came.

"We'll have the chocolate in the drawing room after the dishes have been cleared and washed." Dieter's father could no longer afford a maid. Fortunately, his aunt had accepted the responsibilities of domestic chores gracefully. The war, she would often say, demanded sacrifices of everyone. "You can help me, Anna, by bringing the dishes to the kitchen."

"I'll help, too, Frau Kaufmann," Lili offered.

"Tomas," Ingrid addressed her son, "now would be a good time to show Dieter your surprise."

The ten-year-old pushed his chair from the table and ran from the dining room. "*Danke, Mutti*," he called out as he bounded up the staircase two steps at a time.

Dieter looked at his Aunt Ingrid for some clue. "All I know," she said with a shrug, "is he's been bursting to show you whatever it is since he got home from school."

Tomas entered the dining room, a broad grin on his face. In his hands he clutched a shoebox, which he put on the table. He then opened the lid and took out an object, which he placed on the table. It was a model of a field gun carved in wood.

"Tomas," Dieter said, "this is a wonderful surprise. Where did you get it?"

"From Klaus, a school chum. I gave him my microscope in return."

"Look, Dieter, I've the horses, too!" He took the six animal figures from the box and placed them beside the gun. "And the gun crew!" Four soldier figures joined the horses.

"They're called a detachment, Tomas, not a crew," Dieter corrected.

"And this!" Tomas held up the last piece of the model, a two-wheeled cart with a tongue for hitching the horses.

"That's called a limber," Dieter said. "It's used to carry the ammunition." He took the piece from Tomas. "Here," he said, "they fit together like this." Dieter positioned the horses in three pairs and hooked the gun carriage to the limber, with the barrel pointed to the rear. "There," he said, "a detachment of the German horse artillery, ready to travel."

Tomas seemed disappointed. "But, Dieter, you're in the field artillery."

"The main difference," Dieter explained, "is the number of horses. We use four. The horse artillery requires two more to keep up with the cavalry."

Tomas wanted to know more. "Do the soldiers walk beside the gun?"

"Soldiers in the artillery are called gunners, and, yes, sometimes we walk, or even push, if the terrain is difficult. But most of the time we ride. Our sergeant has his own horse. Each pair of horses has its driver who rides the horse on the left. The rest of us ride on the gun, the corporal and loader on the limber, and my friend Uwe and I on seats in front of the shield on either side of the barrel."

"Do you fire the gun, Dieter?"

"*Nein*, Uwe does that. I'm the gun layer. My job is to sight the gun. I sit here." Dieter pointed behind the shield to the left of the breech. "Uwe sits on the other side. When our sergeant shouts, 'Fire!', Uwe pulls on a lanyard hooked to the firing mechanism and BOOM!" Dieter laughed as Tomas jumped out of his skin.

Suddenly, the young boy's expression turned serious, almost grave.

"What is it, Tomas?" Dieter asked.

"It's something Klaus told me."

"What did he tell you?"

"He said gunners must never let their gun fall into enemy hands." Tomas swallowed hard. "If need be, the last man must give his life to destroy the gun."

Dieter placed a hand on the boy's shoulder. "I won't lie to you, Tomas. What your friend says is true. But you've no reason to worry. Your cousin Dieter belongs to the best gun detachment in the German army. We can take care of ourselves." He punctuated his words with an affectionate squeeze of his cousin's shoulder. The boy seemed reassured.

Dieter watched Tomas and Anna's eyes light up as their mother entered the drawing room, carrying a plate. On it was a piece of Dutch chocolate cut into bite-size pieces.

"We must serve our guest first," Ingrid said, holding out the plate to Lili.

"*Danke*, Frau Kaufman, but *nein*."

"Are you sure? Dieter went to a lot of trouble and expense to get it for us."

"*Ja*, I'm sure he did." Lili turned her head towards Dieter and, for a brief moment, their eyes met. Then Lili looked away towards the piano in the corner of the drawing room. At least this time, Dieter sighed to himself, Lili had chosen to be discreet in expressing her disapproval.

"It hasn't been played since the last time Karl was home on leave," Dieter said. "We would be pleased, Lili, if you would play for us."

"I would love to." Lili rose from her chair and went to the piano. "Do you have a request?" she asked as she sat on the stool.

"Why don't you play something of your choice," Dieter suggested.

“Very well. This is a favourite of mine.’

As the strains of the Brahms’ waltz filled the room, Dieter’s mind wandered back to happier times in the Hannsen household when Karl would play for family and friends.

It wasn’t until Lili finished that Dieter became aware of his father’s presence. Professor Hannsen stood, stooped and frail, in the entrance to the drawing room.

“Would you join us, *Vati*?’

“I thought it was Karl,” he said in a whisper. Then he turned his back on them and returned to his study.

It was Lili who ended the awkward silence. “It’s getting late. I should be going.”

“I’ll see you home,” Dieter said.

“You must come again, Lili,” Aunt Ingrid said.

“*Danke,* Frau Kaufmann. You’re very kind. I hope Professor Hannsen will soon be himself again.”

The walk from the Hannsen home in the suburbs to the old town took about thirty minutes. As the painting of St. George came into view, snow began to fall, the flakes melting as they touched the cobblestones.

As they passed through the gate, Lili stopped and looked up into his eyes. The evening chill had restored some colour to her cheeks. “If I asked you a question, Dieter, would you give me an honest answer?”

He reached out with his hand and gently brushed away a snowflake that had landed on her nose. “Of course.”

“Do you think I’m a prig?”

“A what! Why would you ask such a thing?”

“You know very well why. I saw the look on your face when I turned down the chocolate. You knew exactly why I did it.”

Dieter had to clench his teeth to keep from smiling.

"Whatever do you mean?"

"Oh, stop teasing me." She fixed him with that earnest look that he'd come to find so endearing. "It's just that I believe what we were told when rationing began. That we at home should be prepared to make sacrifices. That no matter what hardship we faced, it would never compare to the suffering ours soldiers had to bear at the front."

"You're someone, Lili, who lives by her principles," Dieter said. "I admire that."

"But tonight my principles cost me a piece of chocolate."

Dieter reached into his pocket and produced the piece he had bought for her.

"Oh, Dieter, you devil!" Lili reached up and threw her arms around his neck.

He gathered her tiny, slender frame with his arms and embraced her tenderly. Through everything, Lili had fought to remain true to her convictions. If only he could match her courage in battle.

A gust of wind surrounded them with a swirl of snowflakes. Dieter felt Lili shiver. "I'd better get you home," he said, "before you catch cold."

At the door to her flat, they stood in silence, not knowing how to say goodbye. Lili offered to see him off in the morning, but Dieter said he hated farewells at train stations.

Instead, he kissed her softly on the cheek. "God be with you, Lili," he said in a whisper.

"And with you, Dieter."

With that, they parted.

Only one room was lit in the Hannsen house by the time Dieter got home. He locked the front door and padded to the foot of the staircase where he stopped and looked to his left towards his father's study. The light from his father's desk lamp illuminated the crack at the foot of the door.

Dieter decided to look in on him. When a light knock brought no response, he opened the door and entered the room. His father was sound asleep on his sofa. Dieter stepped to the desk and switched off the lamp. For a moment he stood in the darkness, his eyes welling up with tears. "I love you, *Vati*," he whispered. "I'll do my best to make you proud of me." Then he left the study, closing the door quietly behind him.

✦

The First World War witnessed the first use of aerial bombings of cities to demoralize civilian populations and break their will to fight on. By 1918 the German High Command was using the twin-engined Gotha and the four-engined R*-plane to bomb London and other targets in southeast England. The "R" stood for "Riese", German for "giant." With a length of almost twenty-two metres and a wingspan of just over forty-two metres, the two-winged* R*-planes were suitably named.*

✦

Chapter 11

February 18, 1918

THE CREW OF R.60 WERE BUSY PREPARING THEIR aircraft for its mission that night. The huge bomber was one of six R-planes stationed at Gontrode, a German airfield in occupied Belgium. One man checked the eighteen tires of its undercarriage. Another climbed a ladder to reach its lower wing where he entered the cockpit to inspect the eight fuel tanks located in its fuselage. A third, on top of its upper starboard wing, checked out one of its four machine guns. A mechanic made final adjustments to one of its port engines.

R.60 had four engines, two on each wing. Each pair was mounted in tandem, one pointing forward, and the other to the rear. This arrangement allowed a front propeller to pull and a rear propeller to push the plane through the air. In between each pair of engines was a special cockpit for a mechanic who could look after minor repairs during flight.

Underneath the fuselage an armourer and three helpers carefully winched a thousand-kilogram bomb into the bomb bay. The armourer turned to an officer standing nearby and said, "This should wake up a few Londoners tonight, eh, Captain Langer."

The comment brought a burst of laughter from the other three men.

"Just make sure you do your job right, Corporal." The officer's voice carried the weight of authority. "It would be a shame to fly all that distance just to drop a dud."

"*Jawohl*, Captain," the man answered, the grin gone from his face. "I checked her out personally. She'll make one big bang. Guaranteed, sir."

The officer glanced up in the direction of the mechanic tinkering with one of the port engines. "I don't relish the thought of going for a swim in the English Channel tonight, Hans."

The mechanic looked up from his work, wiping the grease off his hands with a rag. "Don't worry, Captain. She'll run smoothly now."

Captain Paul Langer was one of a new breed of commander in the bomber squadrons of the German air force. Unlike most of his peers who continued to navigate the aircraft they commanded, Paul chose to fly his. Flying had become his passion.

Paul glanced at the sky. There was no sign of cloud. The meteorologists had promised a clear sky over London tonight. However, Paul knew how unpredictable the weather at this time of year could be. At least it had been warmer than the previous winter — the Turnip Winter.

Without intending to, Paul had brought back the bitter memory of the lowest point of his life. A year ago coal shortages had left the German people with no way to heat their homes in one of the coldest winters on record, and a fungus had destroyed half the potato crop, forcing them to eat a type of turnip grown to feed farm animals. Thousands had died from the cold and lack of nutrition. Among them had been Paul's wife, Therese.

They'd married in the summer of 1912. Paul's prospering import business allowed them to live comfortably in Dahlem, a suburb of Berlin. Sixteen months after the wedding Therese gave birth to their son, Friedrich. Life that autumn of 1913 seemed so full of promise. With the coming of the war, however, their world had started to crumble around them.

At first, Paul's military service had made running

his business difficult, but, with Therese's help, he'd managed until the British naval blockade of Germany took hold. With the ships of the British Royal Navy cutting off trade with the outside world, Germany began to suffer shortages of goods needed for both its military and its people. Paul was one of the blockade's countless victims. Without access to its foreign suppliers, his import business simply ceased to exist. The loss of income forced Therese to sell their home in Dahlem and move into an apartment in Berlin.

Little did Paul and Therese know then that their misfortune was only beginning. A year later, Therese learned that she had tuberculosis. The decline in the general health of the German population brought on by the war had resulted in an increased incidence of the terrible lung disease. Therese had no choice but to make arrangements for Friedrich to stay with Paul's parents. Then she admitted herself to a sanatorium. Before the war, Germany was known worldwide for these special hospitals that treated tuberculosis. However, in the deplorable conditions of the Turnip Winter there was little that could be done for her. Her condition worsened, and she died.

Now, a year later, Paul Langer had still not come to terms with her loss. She had been the only woman he had ever loved. And the only woman, he was convinced, he could ever love. My dear, sweet, lovely Therese, he thought to himself, as the heartache gripped his chest.

As he looked once more at the sky, Paul's anguish was replaced by hatred. There was no doubt in his mind about who was responsible for the tragedy that had befallen him. It was the British blockade that had destroyed his business. It was the British blockade that had deprived Therese of the food she needed to regain her health. It was the British who killed his wife and the mother of his son. Maybe tonight, he thought to himself, some British wives and mothers would die.

Colonel Fotherby and his daughter Meredith entered the Empire's dining room for late afternoon tea and sat at their table without even a glance in Rose's direction. It didn't bother Rose that the colonel refused to acknowledge her existence. What hurt was his refusal to allow Meredith to have anything to do with her. Not even a simple hello was permitted.

"So that's the insufferable colonel," Rose's table companion remarked with a wry smile. Edith Chadwick was a twenty-seven-year-old nursing sister, on leave from the huge complex of military hospitals near the French village of Etaples. Edith and Rose had hit it off from the moment they met. Edith detested the professional snobbery that kept other nursing sisters at a social distance from the V.A.D. auxiliary nurses and ambulance drivers. To Edith, the V.A.D.s were women like herself, trying to do their part with the war effort.

"I tried to apologize to him, Edith, but he refused to listen. He just dismissed me with that infuriating imperious manner of his."

Edith's smile turned sympathetic. "British colonels, Rose, are not used to being given a dressing down by anyone, least of all a woman."

"Oh, Edith, it's not just him. Everyone here, the other guests, the staff, treat me like an outcast."

"Perhaps you're just imagining things."

"No, it's true. If it weren't for my grandfather's money, I have the feeling the management would ask me to leave."

Edith took a sip from her teacup and then set it down on its saucer. "You have to understand, Rose, the war has turned their world topsy-turvy. It wasn't that long ago that a young lady from a good family would never have appeared in public with a man without a chaperone. To do otherwise would have destroyed her reputation. Now the streets, the restaurants, the theatres, are all filled with young women, like yourself, in the company of soldiers. You're seen by some as being …"

Rose completed the sentence, " …Promiscuous?"

Edith nodded.

Is that what you think I am, Edith, a tart?"

"Don't be silly. Of course not. The truth is I envy you, Rose. If only Robert and I had been allowed the freedom you and Liam enjoy." Edith had been engaged to marry a subaltern named Robert Laishley when he was killed in France in 1916 in the terrible Battle of the Somme. "Robert and I were never permitted to be alone. I never knew what it was like to touch, or be touched, by the man I loved."

Rose thought of Liam, and their first embrace and kiss, stolen the previous evening in a secluded part of Hyde Park. His touch had aroused within her a sensual pleasure that had heightened her anticipation of the coming evening, their last together before Liam returned to France. Edith, as always, seemed privy to her thoughts. "If you love each other, Rose, then there is nothing to be ashamed of."

Just then the colonel and Meredith got up from their table and headed for the dining room entrance. As Rose watched them leave, she found herself wondering if Meredith thought she was a fallen woman.

Shortly after sunset, Paul Langer taxied R.60 to the runway at Gontrode and waited for the signal to takeoff. He looked to his left through the main cockpit window to check one last time with Hans. The mechanic's wave told him that the port engines were running smoothly. Paul turned to his right and looked past R.60's co-pilot to the starboard mechanic and got a thumbs-up.

Behind him in the cockpit the navigator, wireless operator and fuel attendant saw to their duties. Even at half-throttle the four engines made a deafening roar and verbal communication in the cockpit was impossible.

Paul preferred to fly with the minimum crew of seven to keep R.60 as light as possible. In the event of an attack by an enemy fighter, the fuel attendant and wireless operator had the additional responsibilities of manning the nose and rear machine guns.

Finally, the signal flare lit up the sky. Paul opened the throttles wide and the power of a thousand horses sent R.60 rolling down the runway. Slowly, the two massive wings lifted the Giant into the sky. Paul circled the airfield and then headed west.

The flight over the English Channel was uneventful. Forty-five minutes from the Belgian coast, Paul looked down through the cockpit window, searching for signs of landfall. They should be over England by now. At this moment, he knew what every man in his crew was wondering. Had they gone off course? Were they lost somewhere over the North Sea? Suddenly, the sky around them lit up. British searchlights were probing the sky, searching for them. They'd made it.

Paul turned around and caught a grin from the navigator. The younger man had done his job. Paul looked past him to the wireless operator and gave him a nod. The operator immediately tapped out a signal on his key, which was picked up by two German receiving stations in Belgium. Using a system of triangulation, the Germans in Belgium quickly calculated R.60's exact location. Within minutes, the wireless operator handed him a piece of paper that read: "30 km east of London."

Paul checked R.60's altitude to make sure that the aircraft was above the enemy's balloon barrage. This form of air defence involved the use of a large number of huge balloons, each tethered to the earth by a heavy steel cable. If R.60 struck one of these cables, the end could be disastrous.

The co-pilot tapped Paul on the arm and pointed out the starboard cockpit window towards the ground in the distance. Paul could see two rows of lights. An airfield had just lit up its runway. Paul's face remained expressionless. A good commander showed no emotion. The fact that the British were sending up a welcoming committee was to be expected. They had to find R.60 first. On another night the airfield would have made a good target. But not this time. The bomb R.60 was carrying was designed for one purpose only: to kill as many British citizens as possible. London remained the primary target.

On Paul's signal, the fuel attendant opened the hatch to the bomb bay and set the bomb's two fuses. One was designed to detonate the bomb on impact; in the event it failed, a time fuse was used as backup. When the fuel attendant finished, the navigator passed between the two pilots and entered a compartment on the nose of the aircraft. From here he would release the bomb. The rest of the crew kept their eyes peeled for enemy fighters and prayed the searchlights didn't find them.

Wisps of cloud suddenly appeared outside the cockpit. Paul cursed the unpredictable English weather.

The lighted runway the co-pilot had spotted was the airfield at Sutton's Farm, part of the British Home Defence. Sutton's Farm had been alerted by telephone by a coastal observation post that had heard the sound of R.60's engines. Within minutes, two of Sutton's

Farm's Sopwith Camel fighter planes were airborne, their pilots searching the night sky for the German intruder.

Chapter 12

Mickey O'Rourke gave them a wave as Rose and Liam came through the door of the pub. They chose a booth along the far wall, away from the regulars who were congregated around the bar. Rose and Liam had come for a late supper after a busy day of touring the city and seeing the musical "Chu Chin Chow", the story of Ali Baba and the forty thieves, set in China.

"Weren't the costumes and scenery spectacular?" Rose asked after the barmaid had taken their order.

Liam nodded, half smiling.

"You're awfully quiet," Rose remarked.

Liam gave that shrug that meant, Rose had come to learn, I'd rather not talk about it. At different times she'd sensed that something was troubling him. She couldn't help but wonder if it had anything to do with her, but had never pressed the matter. She was afraid that he might tell her that he couldn't return the love she felt for him.

A burst of laughter drew their attention to a booth on the opposite side of the pub. Two American soldiers were enjoying a joke over a pint of ale. "Fine lookin' soldiers, your countrymen," Liam commented. "Rumour has it they'll be joinin' us at the front in the spring. You must be proud."

"I'm just glad my country will be finally doing its part."

It was Mickey who served them their food. "How could I forget the pretty lass with a taste for whiskey," he chuckled.

Rose started to respond when she was interrupted by what sounded like distant cracks of thunder. "Is that what I think it is?" Liam asked Mickey.

Mickey nodded. "Anti-aircraft guns. It sounds like the Huns are payin' us another visit tonight."

The anti-aircraft guns they heard were to the east on the city's outskirts. The thickening cloud had made it impossible for the British Home Defence searchlight crews to find R.60, so the gunners were firing blindly into the dark sky, hoping for a lucky hit.

Three thousand metres overhead, Paul Langer and his co-pilot searched for a break in the cloud cover, ignoring the shells that burst around them. One exploded dangerously close, its splinters banging against the fuselage.

Paul looked at his watch. They should have reached London by now. Maybe they'd gone off course. Another commander with less nerve would have dropped the bomb and turned back. But Paul didn't panic. His patience was soon rewarded. Suddenly, the cloud opened up and there below in the moonlight was the grey outline of a city parted by a river. The Thames! London! Paul looked into the nose of the aircraft and signalled the navigator with his hand. The young crewman peered into the bombsight and reached for the lever that released the bomb.

"Is there a bomb shelter nearby?" one of the American soldiers asked Mickey.

"There's one just down the street," he answered, "but I wouldn't bother."

"And why not?" Rose demanded to know.

"About a month ago, a German bomb went through a street grating and exploded in a basement shelter, killin' and maimin' hundreds. There's no safe place, lass."

Rose turned to Liam. "I think we should try to get to the shelter."

"Come on then," he replied.

As they got up to leave, a loud explosion violently shook the whole building, filling the air with the dust. Windows shattered, and bottles and glasses crashed to the floor. "We've been hit!" someone shouted, causing a rush to the door. Rose tried to follow, but Liam took her by the arm and pulled her to the bar. With his free hand he flung several bar stools out of the way. "Lie face down on the floor," he told her.

"But, Liam!" she protested.

"Just do as I say, Rose!"

With a hand on each of her shoulders, Liam pushed Rose face down on the floor at the foot of the bar. Then he lay on top of her, covering her head with his chest. "Liam, please, what are you doing? We've been hit with a bomb. We should — "

"Be still, Rose. That one didn't hit us. But the next one might." He took her right hand in his and squeezed it gently. "It's all right. Trust me. This oak bar will support a lot of weight."

"I'd feel a lot safer in a bomb shelter," Rose persisted, the anger still in her voice.

"To get to a shelter we'd have to expose ourselves," Liam explained.

"Expose ourselves to what?"

"To shell fragments, Rose. Think of those men you've carried in your ambulance, their bodies torn to shreds by exploding shells. I don't want you to end up like them."

Rose's body went limp as she realized what Liam had done. He had used his body to shield hers. "Thank you, Liam," she whispered.

After a few minutes, Liam stood up and helped her to her feet. "Let's take a look outside," he said. The sight from the doorway made them stop in their tracks. About a couple of kilometres away, in the direction of the Empire, the night sky was alight with flames. "Ja-sus," Liam exclaimed, "that had to be one hell of a bomb."

The street outside the pub was empty, except for Mickey who stood shaking his head at the sight of his broken windows. Everyone else, Rose guessed, had fled to the shelter. The glow of the conflagration now filled more of the sky. "Liam," she said with urgency, "they're going to need all the help they can get."

Liam nodded his agreement. They checked the street for a taxi but there was none in sight. Offering her his hand, Liam said, "I guess we'll have to walk."

A split second after the navigator pulled the bomb release switch, R.60 lurched upwards, free of its thousand-kilogram cargo. Paul immediately brought the Giant around in a wide arc, looking to earth to check the location and extent of damage caused by the bomb. He noted with satisfaction the flames that leaped from a point north of the Thames.

R.60 was also being watched.

A thousand metres above, a British Camel pilot had spotted the Giant silhouetted against the glare of the raging fire and was preparing to attack. It was all the young flier could do to get his nervous system under control as the adrenalin rushed through his veins. He gripped the control stick of the Camel with both hands and placed his thumbs on the gun-triggers on the spade-shaped stick top. The triggers connected to two machine guns mounted on the engine cowling directly in front of him. Taking a deep breath, he pushed the control stick forward and sent his airplane into a dive.

The presence of the Camel hadn't gone undetected on board R.60. In his cockpit Hans spotted the flame from the fighter plane's exhaust. On his telegraph key he sent a message to the main cockpit. The lights above Paul flashed: "Enemy fighter sighted."

Hans stood up and reached for a ladder that led to the upper wing. Holding on with all his strength to keep the slipstream from tearing him away into the black abyss of the sky, he climbed up and released a two-door hatch in the upper wing. Then he mounted a platform, which allowed him to poke his head above the upper wing surface. The icy wind lashed at his face and head protected only by goggles and the hood of his flight suit. Mounted on the upper wing was a machine gun which Hans gripped and began firing at the Camel.

The spits of flame from the muzzle of Hans' machine gun startled the British pilot who was convinced that he had caught the Giant crew by surprise. But he held off returning fire, determined to get within closer range.

The belts of bullets that fed into the Camel's machine guns included tracers, bullets that lit up once fired. The tracer bullets allowed the pilot to see the trajectory of his fire at night and make adjustments for greater accuracy. It was the young pilot's first experience using tracers, and he had been warned that they might cause him temporary blindness. It was a risk, however, he was prepared to take if it meant sending the German bomber and its crew to a fiery end.

As he drew closer, he could feel the thud of German bullets striking his aircraft. One shattered his windscreen, narrowly missing his head. But the young pilot continued to resist the urge to fire back. Finally, the outline of the huge bomber loomed in his gun sights.

His two machine guns came to life. Almost instantaneously the flash of the tracer bullets blinded him. In this moment of panic, he had the presence of mind to pull back on the control stick. His Camel roared over the Giant, just missing it by a few metres.

The Camel climbed as the pilot frantically blinked his eyes hoping his sight would return. A short distance away, another British pilot watched in horror as the first Camel suddenly appeared out of the darkness on a collision course with his own.

Walking quickly, Rose and Liam had covered half the distance to the hotel. They were now close enough to hear the roar of the fire and the clang of bells as firemen rushed to the scene.

There were shouts and screams, too, but to Rose they came not from the disaster that was now unfolding just ahead of them, but from the *Lusitania* as it sank off the Irish coast three years ago.

In Rose's mind, the two tragedies, the one triggering the recollection of the other, were quickly fusing into one terrifying ordeal.

Hampered by her long, heavy skirt, she frequently stumbled, just barely regaining her balance. Liam tried to get her to stop and rest but she refused, insisting that she had to go on. People would need help, she told herself. She couldn't let them down.

Just then there was a loud explosion in the sky. They looked up to see the shapes of two aircraft plummeting from the sky in flames.

"Ja-sus, Mary and Joseph!" Liam exclaimed.

The explosion ignited by the colliding Camels violently shook R.60, but the airmen on board the Giant had no time to feel pity for the two enemy pilots who had just perished before their eyes in a ball of fire. While Paul and his co-pilot monitored their instruments for signs of damage from the attack, the navigator plotted their course for home. The rest of the crew continued to watch for other enemy fighters.

The co-pilot was the first to hear the sound and signalled Paul to listen. One of the port engines was misfiring. Some of the bullets from the Camel's machine guns had found their mark. Through the cockpit window Paul could see Hans climbing down the ladder to his cockpit. A minute later the lights above Paul's head flashed a message from Hans. "Aft engine damaged."

As he shut the disabled engine down, Paul caught the concerned look on the co-pilot's face out of the corner of his eye. Once again Paul's face betrayed no emotion. If this is the only thing that goes wrong, he thought to himself, we're home free.

Rose and Liam reached Park Lane a block from the Empire. In the direction of the hotel, clouds of black smoke billowed into the flame-lit sky. What Rose smelled instead was the acrid stench from the *Lusitania's* boilers.

They pushed their way through the throng of people that had gathered in the street until they got close enough to see that Rose's worst fear had come true: The Empire had taken a direct hit.

"Meredith!" she screamed as she ran towards the raging inferno.

"Rose!" Liam called after her. "Are you mad?"

Rose didn't get far before running headlong into the arms of a policeman. "Here now, miss," the policeman said. "Where would you be goin'?"

"Let me through, please. I've got to find Meredith!"

"Meredith?"

"Meredith Fotherby," Rose pleaded. "She's a guest

at the Empire!"

"If she survived the bomb, miss," the policeman explained, "then she's on her way to a hospital, or she's over there." Rose looked across Park Lane to see a group of people huddled together on the edge of Hyde Park. Etched on their faces was a look of sheer terror. These were the fortunate few who had miraculously escaped uninjured.

"Now you must leave this area, miss. It's much too dangerous here, and you're only in the way." The policeman then rushed away in response to a cry for help.

At that moment a fireman passed in front of them, his smoke-smudged face streaked with tears. In his arms was the limp, lifeless body of a young boy. An image flashed through Rose's mind of the body of a child floating faced down in the Celtic Sea.

"Come on, Rose," Liam said, "let's have a look."

Together they hurried across the street to search for Meredith among the group of survivors. There were about sixty of them, most still in their nightclothes. Rose caught sight of a girl about Meredith's height, weeping in the arms of a middle-aged man in his shirtsleeves. But it wasn't her.

Rose continued to call out Meredith's name. A voice finally answered. It was the Empire's doorman, coming towards them, his eyes filled with tears, his voice choked with grief. "Colonel Fotherby and his daughter were on the top floor, Miss Pearce. I'm afraid there's no hope."

"No! No!" Rose shrieked, clasping her head in her hands. "Please, dear God, no! Not again!" All she could think of doing was running to some place safe, far away from this hell that was tormenting her soul. But Liam grabbed hold of her and wouldn't let go. She tried to pull away, but he just held her closer. "Liza!" she wailed. "I'm so sorry! Please forgive me!" Then she broke down into uncontrollable sobs.

✦

Twice on the return flight British searchlights found R.60, but both times the Giant had escaped serious damage. Over the English Channel, the crew could breathe more easily. Even with one engine disabled, Paul was confident the Giant would have no trouble reaching Gontrode. As they crossed the Belgian coastline, he instructed the wireless operator to inform the airfield of their location. A short while later, R.60 was safely on the ground, its crew congratulating each other on a successful mission.

Chapter 13

IT HAD BEEN MONTHS SINCE ROSE RELIVED THE SINKING of the *Lusitania* in her sleep. This time the nightmare was more vivid than ever. The faces were clearer, the screams louder, the cries more heart-rending. Then came that unspeakably terrifying moment when the massive funnel crashed into the sea. "Liza!" Rose screamed as they were sucked into the cavernous cylinder, still spewing sparks and steam like a volcano about to erupt.

"It's all right, Rose" she heard someone say. How can it be all right? She asked herself. Liza is dead, and I'm responsible! She felt a hand on her shoulder, gently shaking her. "Wake up, Rose. It's just a bad dream." It was the same voice, one she recognized. She opened her eyes. There was Liam, sitting on the edge of the bed on which she was lying. Her heart was racing. She tried to speak but her mouth was too dry. Above her a naked light bulb hung from the ceiling, cracked and peeling. The room reeked of mildew and unwashed bodies.

"It's all right, Rose. I'm here. You're not alone."

Her first words were emitted in a hoarse whisper. "Where am I?"

"In a small hotel. I'm afraid it's not what you're used to, but it was the best I could find under the circumstances."

Then Rose remembered them, the two garishly dressed women who had greeted them at the hotel entrance with vulgar remarks and the unsavoury looking man behind the front desk whose leering look had made her skin crawl. "I'm not like those women, Liam," she blurted as she sat up abruptly and reached forward to tug the hem of her skirt over her ankles.

"What women, Rose? What the devil are you talkin' about?"

She turned her head away and stared out the window, its grimy panes streaked by a pelting rain.

"Look at me, Rose."

Reluctantly, she did as he asked. In his face she could see the hurt her words had caused. "Ja-sus, Rose, you think I brought you here to take advantage of you?" This was no attempt to conceal his anger. "You were in distress and needed carin' for. No respectable hotel would take in unmarried man and woman. And the Victoria House's for soldiers only. There was nowhere else to go." He stood up and turned towards the door. "Try to get some more rest. I'll be in the hallway. At daylight, we'll try to find you a better place to stay before I have to catch the train to Folkestone."

"Liam, please don't go," she pleaded. "It was cruel of me to suggest your motive was anything but honourable. It's just that I've never been like this … alone … with a man."

"I'm not just any man, Rose. I'm the one who loves you. Surely you know that."

"Oh, Liam, I wasn't sure. I guess I just needed to hear you say it."

Instead of returning to the bedside, Liam sat on a nearby chair. "Rose," he asked calmly, "who was Liza?'

She'd always vowed to herself she would never talk about what happened that day on the *Lusitania*. Her silence, she was convinced, would help her forget. Now she realized how wrong she'd been. And here was someone who would listen, someone she trusted. "She was a young girl, a Canadian, like you …."

In the street below a lorry door slammed and an engine coughed to life. In the next room a man and a woman shared a joke with a peal of laughter. Rose looked to see if the noises had awakened Liam. But he was still sound asleep, next to her, under the coarse woolen blanket they shared. A glance out the window told her that daylight was near. The rain, she was relieved to see, was letting up. Soon they would have to go. Liam had his train to catch, and she needed to get in touch with Edith who would soon learn of the bombing of the Empire and be frantic with worry.

But Rose was in no hurry to leave. In a few hours, she and Liam would say goodbye, possibly never to see each other again. She wanted desperately to hold on to this moment for as long as she could. She longed for his caress but chose instead to let him sleep. The past eight hours had been as exhausting for him as they'd been for her. She contented herself with reliving in her mind the intimacy they'd shared.

She remembered first his tender words of reassurance about Liza Kincaid.

"You're not alone, Rose. Every soldier knows the feeling of guilt over the loss of a chum. Just before I went on leave, a man named John Latimer was killed, blown to smithereens by a shell. It could have easily been me. I've asked myself many times since, why was

I spared? I don't know the answer to that question, Rose. What I do know is you showed more courage that day on the *Lusitania* than most men I know. You did your best for Liza. Hopefully, one day you will come to accept that."

Then he'd shared with her his secret, the one that had been troubling him so much. "Ever since John died, I've felt I was living on borrowed time, that the next shell will have my name on it. I'm afraid, Rose, afraid to go back to the trenches, afraid of what they'll do to me if I don't."

It was at that moment that Rose knew that it was right. Reaching out with her arms, she invited him to come to her. There was no dread, no shame, only a soon-discovered joy, born of their newly found love. In their embrace, they'd found a sanctuary, if only fleeting, from the violence and death that had darkened their lives.

Now she moved closer to Liam, seeking the warmth of his body. "Just a bit longer, my love," she whispered. "Just a little bit longer."

✦

The German High Command called the planned offensive for the spring of 1918 the "Emperor's Battle", in honour of the German emperor Wilhelm II. Its aim was to deal the British a crushing defeat. With the loss of their ally, the French would then be forced to sue for peace on Germany's terms.

The offensive involved a series of major assaults. The first, code-named Operation Michael, would be launched along an eighty-kilometre stretch of the Western Front held by the British Third and Fifth Armies. It would begin on March 21 at exactly 4:40 a.m.

✦

Chapter 14

March 20, 1918

Dieter Hannsen found it strange not to hear the clomp of horses' hooves and the crunch of ironclad wheels passing over stones. These familiar sounds of a battery of four guns on the move had been muffled by the straw the pioneer battalions had spread over the road.

Seated with Dieter at the rear of Number 3 gun was Uwe Schmidt. Dieter knew Uwe would give anything at that moment to crack a joke or smoke his pipe. But their orders had been clear: no talking or smoking.

And no singing. On the battery's right was a company of storm troopers, marching two abreast. Dieter had been used to hearing German soldiers sing songs of the Fatherland as they marched to the front. But not tonight. Tonight these Germans marched into battle in silence.

Getting one million soldiers and over six thousand guns into position, without alerting the local French populace, was a gigantic, and necessary, undertaking. The success of the attack depended on the element of surprise. The enemy was expecting to face the full might of the German army on the Western Front. However, he didn't know where or when.

The heavy guns were already in place. Their great range allowed them to be positioned as far as twenty kilometres away. The lighter guns, like the 7.7, were being brought closer to the front line where they could support the storm troopers as they advanced across no man's land.

Like all Germans, Dieter honoured the storm troopers as heroes. Specially trained, these young men were the elite of the German infantry. Armed only with submachine guns and grenades, they would serve as the vanguard in the assault on the enemy trenches.

As he looked at the storm troopers marching nearby, Dieter thought of Ernst Bloch and the Battle of Verdun. In the upcoming battle, the storm troopers depended on the gunners for success. Dieter vowed he would not let them down.

Just before dawn, the battery reached its destination, an abandoned farm just south of the ruined and deserted French town of St. Quentin. There was much to be done before daylight. The four detachments busied themselves positioning and camouflaging their guns.

Thirty kilometres to the west, in the French village of Ennemain, a trumpeter blew the call that every soldier had learned to hate. The five hundred men of Lord Strathcona's Horse, bedded in cellars, attics and stables, grumbled and cursed at the sound of reveille. The Strathconas shared the village with the Royal Canadian Dragoons. The Fort Garry Horse, the third regiment of the Canadian Cavalry Brigade, was billeted nearby.

The Brigade had been withdrawn to the rear to act as a reserve in the event the Germans attacked. Most of the time was spent exercising the horses and building fortifications. This day would be no different. First the horses were fed, watered and groomed, the saddles were scrubbed, and the stables were cleaned. Then, after a breakfast of bully beef, biscuits and tea, work parties were formed to repair trenches.

Liam Cassidy was never happier as a soldier than he was on days like this. Liam was no stranger to hard work. Since he was fifteen, he'd laboured in the lumber camps and sawmills of the Ottawa Valley to help support his mother and sister. Working with the horses reminded him of the times his father had taken him for rides on the wagons loaded with freshly sawn lumber.

Liam had another reason for welcoming the busy routine. It helped take his mind off the fear that continued to gnaw away at his insides, the fear that his number was up, that when the fighting resumed he was going to die.

The company of friends served the same purpose. In the afternoon, he joined a number of Strathconas and Dragoons at the football pitch to watch their regimental teams play a friendly match. Football was very popular among the men of the Brigade who'd come from the British Isles. Two of the Strathconas's best players were Reg Longley, "C" Squadron's trumpeter, and Wilf Hazel. Both men had emigrated to Canada from England before the war. Reg found a home in Brandon, Manitoba, while Wilf took up farming in Saskatchewan.

The match was a spirited affair. The only goal came when Reg headed a well-placed corner kick from Wilf passed the Dragoon keeper. The cheering Strathconas mobbed their team. Two of them hoisted Reg on to their shoulders where he was given three resounding hurrahs. On the third, everyone threw his cap into the air.

"Liam," Reg called out as he was lowered to the ground, "you should give football a try."

"Thanks," Liam replied, "but I think I'll stick to hockey."

"I tried skating once," Wilf said, joining the banter, "but I spent the whole time on my backside."

Everyone laughed, Wilf the loudest. He could always be counted on for a joke, even one at his own expense.

With the game over, the men returned to their

billets to find that the mail had arrived. There was a letter for Liam from Rose. He found some privacy in a corner of the stable his troop called home and sat down and read it. It was her second letter since that morning she saw him off at London's Victoria Station a month ago. Like her first, it was informative, humorous and, above all, intimate. His one letter, on the other hand, was more like a cablegram, short and to the point. Liam found it hard to express his feelings for Rose in the written word. He longed to be with her again to show her how much he loved her.

"A letter from a sweetheart?"

Liam looked up to see Alex MacNeil, a broad grin on his face. He hadn't seen much of his friend since his promotion to corporal and transfer to Fred Harvey's 2nd Troop. Lieutenant Harvey was the regiment's only recipient of the Victoria Cross. He had won the coveted award for valour for capturing a German machine gun emplacement single-handedly.

Liam laughed. "Is it that obvious?"

"You've that swooned look of a man in love."

"Someone I met when I was on leave," Liam explained as he put the letter into the breast pocket of his tunic.

"How about some supper at Jacques'?" Alex asked. Jacques was a villager who ran a tavern, what the French called an *estaminet*, out of his house. His food was a definite improvement over army rations.

"Only if you're payin'," Liam answered. "You can afford it on a corporal's pay."

At the *estaminet*, Liam and Alex were joined by Wilf, Reg and another Manitoban named George Henderson. George had been studying history at university in Winnipeg when he decided to enlist. A quiet, introspective young man, he spent much of his free time reading.

They ordered eggs, chips and a loaf of French bread. Liam asked for chicory coffee; the others decided to share a bottle of wine. As Reg filled his glass, Wilf said, "You're not old enough to be drinking that stuff." Reg, whose boyish looks belied his twenty-one years, was used to this good-natured ribbing, and he dismissed Wilf's comment with a laugh.

The conversation turned to the football game and the latest news from Canada. At one point Wilf asked George what he was reading lately.

"A book about the Peloponnesian War," George answered, "It took place in ancient times. Greek fought Greek for twenty-seven years until all of Greece was destroyed."

Liam stared, grim-faced, at the empty wine bottle. "Just like this damn war," he said. "The killin' will go on for years until there is no one left alive."

"Not if the Germans have anything to say about it," Reg interjected. "They're looking to end it all before the Yanks get here. They'll try soon, to be sure. The only question's where?" He turned to Alex who was seated to his right. "What's your guess, Corporal?"

There was no hesitation to Alex's reply. "If I were the Hun, I'd have a go at the Fifth Army." The heavy losses at the Battle of Passchendaele the previous autumn had left the British Fifth Army undermanned and dependent on inexperienced recruits. All it had in reserve were six cavalry brigades. The Canadians were one of them.

Wilf spoke up. "So, Corporal, you think we'll be in the thick of it."

Alex drained his wine glass and pushed his chair from the table. "Aye, laddie," he said as he stood up to leave, "You mark my words."

Reg, George and Wilf joined Alex as he headed for

the door. Liam, however, remained seated at the table. Suddenly he felt very tired. Bone weary was a better way of putting it. His mood was becoming gloomier, and there was nothing he could do to stop it.

The others waited for him. "Are you all right, laddie?" Alex asked.

"Yeah, I'm fine," Liam replied. "You fellas go on. I'll be along later."

After they'd left, Liam called out to Jacques. "Do you have anything stronger to drink than that wine?"

The tavern keeper nodded and reached behind the counter. "*Oui, monsieur*," he replied. "If you have the money, I've just what you're looking for."

Dieter's sergeant was a tough disciplinarian who demanded nothing short of perfection of his detachment. While the rest of the battery ate supper, his gunners prepared and checked their gun for action.

One of the drivers and the loader laboured to clean the barrel with a rod and brush. The other driver was off feeding the horses. Near the rear of the gun, the corporal made one final check of the ammunition. In one stack were shells containing a high explosive. The shells in the other were marked with a green cross, identifying phosgene, a highly toxic gas.

Uwe took his seat on the left side of the gun behind the shield. With his right hand he gripped a lever on top of the breech. As he pulled it towards him, then pushed it away, he watched to make sure the crank, the part that opened and closed the breech, worked properly. Next, he turned his attention to the firing mechanism. First he switched it from "safety" to "fire." Then he took from around his neck a lanyard made of a short length of cord with a steel hook tied at one end. He hooked the lanyard onto the firing mechanism and, with his left hand, gave the cord a yank. The familiar snapping sound of the mechanism working properly brought a smile to his face. Uwe took great pride in his job. No matter how foul and muddy the conditions, his responsibility was to keep the breech clean and well oiled. Otherwise the gun wouldn't fire.

Seated to Uwe's left, on the other side of the breech, Dieter held his right eye to the gun sight. As the gun layer, his job was to "lay" the gun on target.

"Is the range set correctly, Hannsen?"

Dieter had set the range by elevating the barrel. "*Jawohl*, Sergeant," Dieter answered immediately. "Twenty-five degrees elevation."

"Enough German soldiers will be dying in a few hours at the hands of the enemy," the sergeant added. "They don't need to be killed by their own creeping barrage."

No one understood the dangers of a creeping barrage better than the gun layer. Following the opening bombardment, the plan called for hundreds of batteries of 7.7s to lay down a concentrated area of shellfire three hundred metres ahead of the advancing storm troopers. The purpose of the barrage was to destroy anything and anyone that had survived the heavy guns. To keep pace with the storm troopers, the barrage would pause every five minutes to allow the gun layers to re-sight their guns at the new range. In this way the barrage "crept" across the battlefield.

Dieter's battery had spent hours perfecting the creeping barrage at a training facility that simulated battle conditions by using live ammunition. But in the heat of real battle the risk of human error was higher. An incorrect range setting could have tragic consequences. Shells that fell short could kill their own infantry.

"You can count on me, Sergeant," Dieter replied confidently.

The sergeant nodded and then instructed the detachment to get some food and rest. "This may be your last chance to eat or sleep for days."

The gunners finally ate their supper in silence, each lost in his own thoughts. These men, Dieter now realized more than ever, had become his brothers. It was a comradeship nurtured in training. Now it would be forged in battle. Tomorrow they would do their part to drive the British into the sea.

Liam stared at the label on the bottle. The only French word he recognized was *cognac*. The bottle of French brandy had emptied his pocket of francs. Liam splashed some of the potent amber liquid into a small glass.

He remembered his first drink. It was on a night that he scored the winning goal in his first game for a team in a neighbourhood league. Afterwards, in the change room, they'd passed a bottle around to celebrate. He'd been only sixteen years old.

Hockey had offered an escape from the drudgery of his father's working class existence. His contract with the Senators put more money in his pocket than he'd ever seen in his life. Even more important was the respect that came with wearing the Senators' uniform. Strangers stopped him in the street and wished him well. Young boys looked up to him in awe. For the first time in his life, Liam felt truly happy.

Then the war had cast its dark cloud over this promising future. As the casualty lists grew longer, pressure had mounted on young, single men to enlist. Liam had considered joining up but knew his mother would be dead set against it. No son of hers was going to die fighting in a British war.

Defying his mother was not something he even wanted to consider. In the years after his father's death, as he'd grown from boy to man, she'd stood by him, providing for him and guiding him with a firm, but loving, hand. Without her, Liam was convinced, he would have come to no good.

However, there had been a price to pay for not enlisting. Those who'd wished him well now ignored him. And the adoration soon turned to scorn. For Liam, the low point had come that winter morning on Parliament Hill. *I despise you.* The woman's denunciation had shaken him to the very core of his being.

Liam lifted the glass of cognac and held it in his hand.

That night, after the confrontation with the woman on the Hill, he'd gone to Flannagan's Tavern to drink himself into a stupor. His mother, ignoring a law that prohibited women from entering saloons, had shown up to bring him home.

Later, over a mug of coffee at the kitchen table, she explained that she'd found out about the incident with the white feather that afternoon. News, she reminded her son, travelled quickly in the Flats. When Liam hadn't shown up for supper, she'd guessed he was at Flannagan's and had gone to fetch him home.

"That woman's grief has made her bitter, Liam," his mother said as she re-filled his mug. "One day she'll regret what she did to you."

At first Liam said nothing. He'd already made up his mind to enlist, and he sensed that his mother knew it. When he finally spoke, he knew his words would hurt her deeply. "It's somethin' I must do, Mum," he said. "I couldn't hold me head high if I didn't go."

Liam knew his mother had her arguments ready: other players for the Senators hadn't joined up; Mrs. O'Leary's son had stayed home to look after her; Liam's father would turn over in his grave if he knew his son was going to fight for Britain. Instead, she remained silent.

"You'll be looked after, Mum. I'll see to it, you know I will."

A tear trickled down her cheek. "It's not that Liam. Losin' me husband was hard enough. I couldn't bear to lose me son."

Liam reached across the table and took his mother's hands in his. "I'll be fine, Mum," he said, "don't worry." That afternoon, he told her, he'd gone to see one of the Senators' wealthy backers in his plush office on Wellington Street. The man had promised to use his influence to get Liam into Lord Strathcona's Horse. "There isn't much use for the cavalry in trench warfare," Liam concluded. "With any luck I'll come out of this in one piece."

In the end, she gave him her blessing. There was, however, one condition. "Ye must make yeer mother a promise, Liam. Ye must promise me never to drink again."

Liam stared at the glass of cognac still in his hand.

A promise to his mother was a promise to be kept.

He set the glass down, got up from the table and walked out of the *estaminet* into the night.

At exactly 4:40 a.m. a large white rocket lit up the sky over St. Quentin. On cue, the German heavy guns erupted in a deafening, earthshaking clap of thunder. The gunners of Dieter's detachment huddled together, their ears plugged with wads of cotton, as the shells passed overhead with the roar of a thousand freight trains.

For five hours, the bombardment slammed into the lines of the British Fifth Army, destroying trenches and dugouts, blowing up ammunition dumps, shattering phone lines, knocking out guns, and saturating the entire area with phosgene gas. Then, as suddenly as it began, it ceased.

"Take post!" the sergeant commanded.

In seconds, Number 3 gun was ready, a high explosive shell loaded in the breech. The sergeant, his right arm raised, waited for the order from the officer commanding the battery. Five kilometres away, the shrieks of hundreds of whistles signalled the storm troopers to begin their attack.

The order was given. The sergeant dropped his arm and shouted, "Fire!"

The men of the Canadian Cavalry Brigade had been awakened by the roar of the German bombardment. Shortly after it ceased, the Brigade was given the order to prepare for battle: "Stand to your horses."

Each man saddled his horse. A scabbard strapped at the rear left side of the saddle held his sword. His rifle, the Short Magazine Lee Enfield, was kept in a boot on the rear right side. Ammunition for the rifle was stored in the pouches of a bandolier, slung over his left shoulder. A second bandolier was hooked around his horse's neck. Over the man's right shoulder hung a haversack containing a respirator that would be strapped to his face in the event of a gas attack. In a separate haversack fastened to the saddle was a respirator for his horse.

Then came word that there would be a delay. The men loosened the saddle cinches and sat on the ground in front of their horses to wait.

"That's all we do in the army," Wilf grumbled, "hurry up and wait."

"What's your hurry?" said George. "Our time will come soon enough."

Time for what? Liam wondered. To fight? Or to die?

It was late afternoon before their orders finally came. The Strathconas, the Dragoons and the Fort Garrys mounted their horses and rode east to face the enemy.

✦

The Canadian cavalrymen could do little to help stop the massive German assault. On March 24, they joined the British Fifth Army in retreat. By March 29, the Germans had advanced fifty kilometres, taking tens of thousands of prisoners, and were threatening to capture the French city of Amiens. To defend Amiens, the British threw together a patchwork collection of units that included the battle-scarred Canadian Cavalry Brigade.

Late in the evening of March 29, the Brigade encamped ten kilometres southeast of Amiens. All three regiments had suffered casualties since the start of the German offensive. The three Strathcona squadrons were down to one hundred men each. Before these exhausted survivors could get some sleep, their horses had to be unsaddled and fed.

At that moment, eight kilometres to the east, a battalion of eight hundred soldiers from the German state of Saxony was occupying Moreuil Wood, a tree-covered ridge near the French hamlet of Castel. From the ridge, the Saxons could look down into the valley at the rail line that led south to Paris. Severing this rail line was an important step in the German plan to capture Amiens.

✦

Chapter 15

March 30, 1918

By first light, the men of the Canadian Cavalry Brigade, enveloped in a cold mist, were standing to their horses, ready to move out. Then came word that there would be a delay.

To pass the time, the Scotsmen in Liam Cassidy's squadron sang songs from their homeland. It was Alex MacNeil's pure tenor voice that left the men choked with emotion.

I'm leaving Loch Leven,
I'm leaving this heaven,
I'm going to a foreign shore
My fortune to seek.

As he listened, Liam thought of his parents leaving the poverty of Ireland to build a new life in Canada. He wondered what his father would say if he knew his only surviving son had returned to Europe to face death on the battlefields of France.

Finally, after a three hour wait, Gordon Flowerdew gave the order to "C" Squadron: "Get mounted, boys. This is it!"

The inhabitants of Castel were long gone, the homes and shops abandoned to the rats. As the men of Lord Strathcona's Horse rode two abreast down the main street, Liam spotted a broken rocking horse lying in the gutter. The sounds of children playing had been replaced by the neighing of horses, the clatter of hooves on cobblestones, and the squeaking of saddles and harnesses.

The view ahead was obstructed by trees that lined the banks of the river that flowed through the valley on the eastern edge of the hamlet. From beyond the trees came the sound of rifle and machine gun fire. The Royal Canadian Dragoons, the Brigade's senior regiment, were already in the thick of the battle.

It was not until they reached the bridge that spanned the river that the Strathconas got their first look at the battlefield. About two kilometres away, the valley rose gently to a ridge that was covered by a large stand of trees, leafless in the early spring. It was called, the men had been told, Moreuil Wood.

Just beyond the bridge was a rail line. As he crossed the tracks, Liam noticed a handful of French soldiers off to one side, digging rifle pits. The soldiers stopped to wave and cheer the Canadians on.

"I bet they're glad to see us," remarked Wilf, who was riding on Liam's right.

Near the northwest corner of Moreuil Wood, Liam could barely make out a red pennant fluttering in the wind. Here, Jack Seely, the Brigade's commanding officer, had set up his headquarters. General Seely had made the decision to drive the Germans from Moreuil Wood. At his order, the Dragoons had begun the attack. Now the general sent word for Lord Strathcona's Horse to advance.

As the three squadron trumpeters sounded the command, the Strathconas urged their horses into a canter and rode up the slope of the valley to join the battle.

Five kilometres to the east, Dieter Hannsen's gun detachment advanced slowly along a road choked with German infantry. Mounted on his horse, Dieter's sergeant peered through binoculars, searching ahead for the rest of the battery. Earlier that morning Number 3 gun had fallen behind when one of its horses had thrown a shoe. Of greater concern to the sergeant were the sounds of a battle coming from a wooded area just ahead.

Seated at the rear, Dieter and Uwe found themselves conversing with the soldiers marching behind the gun. They were fellow Schwarzwalders, men from the Black Forest.

"What town?" Dieter called out to one of them.

"Lahr." Came the answer. "And you?"

"Freiburg."

"What can you tell us?" Uwe asked.

The soldier from Lahr shrugged. "All I know is we're supposed to relieve the Saxons in that forest up ahead."

"Sounds like you're in for a warm welcome."

The soldier nodded grimly.

Minutes later Number 3 gun came to a sudden halt. Dieter and Uwe turned to see an infantry officer on foot, pointing towards the woods as he barked out orders to the sergeant. The sergeant then turned and signalled the drivers to follow him. The drivers turned the horses off the road and, using their whips, urged them forward across a farmer's field. The men riding on the gun and the limber grabbed hold of their handrails to keep from being thrown from their seats.

Near a slight hollow about four hundred metres from the northeast corner of the woods, the sergeant reined in his horse and waited for the gun to catch up. Here, his detachment would find some protection from enemy fire. At the sergeant's signal, the drivers wheeled the horses about and brought the gun into the hollow, with its barrel now pointing towards a gap between the northeast corner of the woods and a smaller stand of trees just to the north.

When they reached the point where he wanted the gun unlimbered, the sergeant ordered: "Halt! Action rear!" As the drivers brought the horses to a halt, the gunners jumped down from their seats into action. Dieter and Uwe set the brakes on the wheels of the gun, while the corporal and the loader unhooked the gun from the limber and set it down on its trail.

"There are reports of enemy tanks in the area," the sergeant explained as the gunners prepared the gun for action. "They may come through that gap to attack our right flank. Sight on that tall tree in the middle of the gap."

Dieter repeated the sergeant's directions to ensure that he had the right aiming point before fetching the gunsight from a tin box attached to the shield. Then he proceeded to sight and level the gun as ordered.

At the same time, Uwe removed the waxed canvas covers from the muzzle and the breech and checked the breech mechanism, while the corporal and loader unloaded the ammunition from the limber and stacked it to the right of the trail. In addition to armour-piercing shells for tanks, the corporal included some shrapnel and high explosive rounds. In battle it was always wise to prepare for the unexpected.

Within two minutes Number 3 gun was ready for action. The sergeant signalled the drivers to take the limber and the horses to safety fifty metres to the rear.

At the northwest corner of Moreuil Wood, General Seely gave the Strathconas their orders.

"B" Squadron was to dismount and enter the northern face of the wood in support of the two squadrons of Dragoons who were already in a bitter fight. "A" Squadron was to wait in reserve. "C" Squadron was told to remain mounted. They had the most dangerous mission. The general ordered Gordon Flowerdew to lead his men around the northeast corner and cut off enemy reinforcements trying to enter the woods from the east.

Flowerdew saluted. "It's a splendid moment, sir. I will try not to fail you."

Looking calm and confident, Flowerdew rode back to the squadron and ordered Fred Harvey to take 2nd Troop ahead and secure the northeast corner. As he watched Harvey's troop gallop off, Liam wondered if he would see Alex MacNeil alive again.

Flowerdew followed with the three remaining troops, riding two abreast. Along the way they came across the bodies of Dragoons, lying crumpled on the ground. Liam tried not to think about them, or the sound of stray bullets — a "crack" followed by a "thump" — coming from the woods to his right. A nervous rider made for a skittish horse.

Suddenly, a man up ahead slumped in his saddle. Then he fell to the ground with a thud. A stray bullet had found a target. "C" Squadron kept moving. There was no time to stop.

Dieter studied the lay of the land in the target area. A draw appeared to extend from behind the corner of the larger wood on the left into the gap. This shallow valley could provide cover for an enemy tank until it climbed up on the higher ground where it would come face to face with Number 3 gun. It would be no match, Dieter told himself, against the armour-piercing shell now loaded in the breech.

Movement to the left of the gap caught Dieter's attention. On the high ground about three hundred metres away, German soldiers were withdrawing from the wood and forming up into two lines. The first was about three hundred metres from the draw, the other about one hundred metres farther back.

"One hundred and twenty men," Dieter heard the sergeant say. "A full company. And they have heavy machine guns. With our help they should be able to deal with any threat from the gap."

Then Uwe tapped Dieter on the shoulder and pointed behind them. The Schwarzwalders were moving up as reinforcements. Help was on its way.

As the morning sun peered through the clouds, Gordon Flowerdew sent his three troops into the draw, where they were afforded some protection, while he rode to the northeast corner of the wood to confer with Fred Harvey. The two officers agreed on what to do next. Harvey's men would drive the Germans in front of them out of the woods into the open on the east side of the woods where Flowerdew's men would cut them down in a mounted charge. It was the moment a cavalryman had trained for — the pursuit of foot soldiers in the open field.

Flowerdew galloped back to the draw where he shouted the order, "Loosen your swords!" Liam reached for the grip of his sword and gave it a short pull to make sure it was free in its scabbard. Then Flowerdew led his men farther along the draw before they spurred their horses up onto the high ground.

What Liam saw turned the blood in his veins ice-cold and his bowels to jelly. Ja-sus, he thought, they're waitin' for us!

Flowerdew drew his sword and turned in his saddle. "It's a charge, boys!" he called out. "It's a charge!"

Reg Longley brought his trumpet to his lips but was felled by enemy bullets before he could sound the call. The rest of the squadron followed Flowerdew into a hail of gunfire.

Dieter's jaw dropped in astonishment. Suddenly, a column of enemy cavalry emerged from the draw and wheeled right in two ranks. Howling like savages, the horsemen charged the first line of German infantry, swords drawn and held straight ahead as extensions of their right arms.

"Cavalry in the open!" the sergeant shouted. "Get rid of that armour-piercing round! Fire!"

Uwe yanked his lanyard, igniting the propellant in the shell casing with an ear-splitting boom that kicked the gun back in recoil. As the now useless armour-piercing projectile passed harmlessly over the heads of the charging horsemen, the loader was reaching for a round of deadly shrapnel from the pile of shells. Uwe opened the breech, ejecting the smoking casing and filling the air with the acrid smell of burnt powder.

"Take post to lay!" the sergeant ordered. "Trail right!"

As Dieter released the left brake, the corporal and one of the drivers, who had come to help, lifted the trail and swung it to the right, bringing the gun to bear on the charging cavalry to the left. Dieter quickly found the horsemen in the gunsight and began tracking them with the traverse hand wheel. At this distance he could actually see their faces.

The sergeant called out the range: "Three hundred metres! Engage!"

With his other hand Dieter adjusted the elevation of the barrel. The loader was ready with a shrapnel shell cradled in his left arm. With his right hand he turned the fuse to the minimum setting. Then he shoved the shell into the breech.

"On!" Dieter called out.

"Ready!" bellowed Uwe.

"Fire!" the sergeant commanded.

Dieter pulled his head back from the sight to protect his eye from the gun's recoil.

BOOM!

To help absorb the recoil, the corporal leaned on the hand spike, directing the spade at the end of the trail into the ground. A fraction of a second later, the shell exploded in the air just metres from the first line of cavalry. BLAM! Hundreds of marble-sized balls shredded a dozen Canadians and their horses.

"Range two hundred! Load!" the sergeant screamed. The steps were repeated. BOOM! BLAM!

A second blast of shrapnel cut down ten more horses and their riders.

Deafened by the exploding shells, Liam saw the horses in front of him stumble, then fall. God help us, he thought, as his charger jumped over a stricken horse and rider. The first enemy soldier Liam encountered wielded his empty rifle like a club. What he'd done a hundred times in training to a straw-filled dummy, he now did to a human being. As he rode past the German, he plunged his sword down through the soft tissue near the man's neck into his chest cavity, piercing his heart. Holding on to the grip with all his strength, Liam allowed the forward motion of his horse to pull the sword free.

Suddenly, his horse reared and then bolted to the left. Liam tried with all his strength to rein in the terrified animal as it raced out of control towards a German field gun, sheltered in a shallow depression three hundred metres away.

"Enemy horseman!" Dieter's sergeant shouted above the din of the battle.

Dieter rose from his seat and looked over the gun shield. What he saw made him choke on his heart. Bearing down on the detachment was a cavalryman, his horse in full gallop, its hooves throwing up clumps of mud.

We're unarmed, was Dieter's first thought, except for the sergeant who, he was relieved to see, had already drawn his revolver and was taking aim. Not far away, a platoon of Schwarzwalders had been alerted to the threat and was opening fire.

Dieter froze where he stood, his eyes now riveted on the charging horse, just a hundred metres away. The rider leaned forward in the saddle, trying desperately to make himself a smaller target. On they came, horse and man, seemingly invincible to the withering gunfire. Then, just fifteen metres from the gun, the horse tumbled forward, then rolled on its left side, pinning the rider's leg. As the man tried desperately to free himself, the sergeant aimed his revolver and fired. Dieter winced as the bullet struck the cavalryman, driving him on to his back with such force that he lost his helmet.

It was only then that Dieter realized that his body was trembling. Ashamed, he stole a quick glance at Uwe, but his friend hadn't noticed. Uwe instead was staring at the battlefield, now shrouded with wisps of smoke and littered with dead and dying men, clad in both German grey and enemy khaki. In the distance Dieter spotted a horse, hobbling about, its right hind leg sheared off above the knee. To the animal's left, a cavalryman helped a wounded comrade.

Both men could see that the cavalry charge had given the advantage to the enemy who now appeared to be gaining the upper hand in the wood. To their rear, the Schwarzwalders, fearing the arrival of more horsemen, began to withdraw. Their sergeant, however, was an experienced veteran who didn't panic easily. Surveying the battlefield through his binoculars, he searched out another target. "There!" he shouted, pointing to the northeast corner of the wood where enemy soldiers were emerging into the open and firing at the Germans withdrawing from the woods to the south. "Trail left!"

Uwe immediately released the brake on the right wheel. Then the corporal and the driver lifted the trail to the left, rotating the gun to point at the new target. Within seconds the detachment was directing shellfire at Fred Harvey and his troop of Strathconas, forcing them to seek cover.

As the German shrapnel began to take its toll, Lieutenant Harvey turned to the one man who could save them. "Corporal MacNeil!" he shouted above the din of the battle. "Do something about that gun!"

Alex moved quickly out of the woods on to the battlefield, sprinting full out until he found cover behind a dead Canadian horse about three hundred and fifty metres from the German gun. From here he had a clear view of four of the gunners, exposed from the waist up. The distance was well within the Lee Enfield's range for an accurate shot. Alex adjusted the back sight and, lining it up with the foresight, took aim at the detachment's commander, the man with the binoculars. He was the first to die. It wasn't long before the other three were dispatched. Now Alex waited patiently for the remaining gunners to poke their heads above the shield.

Liam had been sure he was going to die, but the next bullet, the one that would finish him off, never came. The first one had slammed into his right shoulder with the force of a mule kick. So far there was little pain, but he knew from experience that that wouldn't last for long. His lower left leg, pinned beneath the horse, he was sure was broken. His body felt cold, his mouth dry, the symptoms, he recognized, of shock.

Liam continued to lie still, afraid to move. The German gunners, he figured, had either forgotten about him or thought he was dead. For several minutes he'd heard their voices, shouting out in German the commands of their drill as they continued to fire their gun. Now the gun was silent.

Slowly, Liam turned his head to see what had happened. What came into view was the gun, a short distance away, turned so that he could see two of the gunners huddled behind the shield. The others lay dead, a marksman's work, probably Alex MacNeil. Now Liam had to try to finish the job. His rifle was still in its boot. If only he could reach it.

"We must save the gun!" Uwe shouted.

Dieter turned and looked at the German soldiers still withdrawing from the woods under enemy fire. "No!" he replied. "We must help them!"

"We've done all we can for them, Dieter! There're only two of us left. Our duty now is to save the gun!"

Not waiting for an answer, Uwe ran off to help the other driver bring up the limber and the horses. He didn't get ten metres before a bullet from Alex's rifle struck him between the shoulders, shattering his spine.

Dieter stared in horror at his friend's body lying in the mud. Then he looked up to see the driver frantically cutting his horse out of its traces. Panic-stricken, the man rode off, abandoning Dieter and the gun.

Dieter was the last man. Alone he could not save the gun. There was only one thing left to do.

The last man must give his life to destroy the gun.

For a brief moment he allowed himself to think of his family and of Lili. He prayed that some good would come to them from all this suffering. Then he stared at the stack of shells on the other side of the trail. Two would be needed. One rammed down the muzzle; the other to be fired from the breech. The resulting explosion would do the job.

Dieter crawled over the trail to Uwe's vacated post, carefully keeping below the shield.

As he lunged for a shell, a bullet grazed his steel helmet, knocking it from his head. Safely back behind the shield, he shoved the shell into the breech and closed it.

One more was needed for the muzzle. This time Dieter knew the enemy marksman wouldn't miss. But he had to try. It was his duty. The enemy must never be allowed to turn the gun against German soldiers.

It was then that he noticed the fallen enemy cavalryman. The movement of his hand was the first thing to catch his eye. He seemed to be reaching out for help.

Then their eyes met. And Dieter realized who it was.

He knew immediately what he had to do. God had given him a second chance.

Alex watched as the German, now helmetless, reappeared from the other side of the gun and ran a short distance before appearing to drop to his knees. For a brief moment he wondered what the man was up to, but it was a question quickly dismissed from his mind. He could see the man's head. That's all he needed. He acquired the target in the rifle's sights and squeezed the trigger.

Crack!

"One more Hun," he spat, "sent to Hell."

✦

The Battle of Moreuil Wood continued into the late afternoon. By evening, the Canadian Cavalry Brigade, with the help of British cavalry units, had won its objective. The cost, however, had been high. The Strathconas alone had one hundred and fifty-seven men killed or wounded. The next morning, only eleven men and thirty-six horses from Flowerdew's squadron stood up for muster. Among those killed in the charge were Privates Reginald Longley, Wilfred Hazel and George Henderson. Gordon Flowerdew died a short while later from his wounds.

The only hope for a soldier whose injuries prevented him from walking or crawling from the battlefield were the stretcher-bearers. These brave men risked their lives to carry the wounded to aid posts and dressing stations that were equipped to provide basic medical care. More serious cases were transported by truck to casualty clearing stations for further treatment. From there they were taken, first by train and then by ambulance, to the huge complex of hospitals near the French fishing village of Etaples. These ambulances were driven by the women of the Voluntary Aid Detachment.

✦

Chapter 16

April 2, 1918

Rose Pearce watched in horror as wounded British soldiers, borne on stretchers, were lifted from the train and loaded into her ambulance. Dressings that should have been clean were caked in blood and filth. Shattered limbs were crudely splinted with bandages instead of plaster casts. Unable to cope with the deluge of casualties caused by the German offensive, the casualty clearing stations were simply loading the wounded on the hospital trains bound for Etaples.

Unable to look anymore, Rose turned her head to the east where the artillery thundered and the muzzle flashes lit up the night sky. Rumours were rampant. The Germans, said some, had taken Amiens. Others believed the war was lost.

Of one thing Rose was certain: the Western Front was on her doorstep, and she was afraid. Fear and lack of sleep had taken their heavy toll on her body. In the last two days she'd slept only a few hours. Thankfully, this was her last convoy before she was relieved.

It was an hour's drive from the railway station to Number 24 General Hospital, one of the many hospitals that had been built near Etaples. These hospitals weren't the multi-storey buildings soldiers knew back home, but rather collections of wooden huts and marquees strung out in rows.

The dirt road to Number 24 was slick with mud and riddled with water-filled potholes, some of which Rose found impossible to avoid at night. She cringed at the moans and cries of the wounded men in her care. At the hospital reception area, orderlies unloaded her ambulance. Nearby, other wounded men waited on their stretchers to be evacuated to a ship in Boulogne for transportation to Britain.

Before going off duty, Rose had to clean up her ambulance for the next driver. Finally, at two o'clock in the morning, she made her way to the hut where she slept. As she unbuttoned her coat, her eye caught sight of something on her pillow. It was note from Edith Chadwick. It read: "Your Canadian is in my ward." Not bothering to re-button her coat, Rose rushed back to the hospital.

What never ceased to amaze Rose about Edith was her calm, resolute demeanour. It never wavered no matter how difficult the problem or how major the crisis. Even at this moment, when her ward resembled an aid post near the front, overflowing with grievously wounded men, she seemed unruffled and in control. "I'm glad you got my note, Rose" she said, stepping around a pile of torn, mud-caked uniforms, stained black with blood. "He's scheduled to be evacuated soon. As you can see, we desperately need the beds."

Rose tried to catch her breath. "How is he, Edith?"

"A fractured tibia and a bullet wound to his shoulder. He's lost a great deal of blood, but fortunately there's no sign of infection. The doctor thinks he should mend."

"May I see him?"

Edith nodded. "The last bed on the right. Just try not to wake him. He needs his rest."

"Thank you, Edith. You're a good friend."

Edith reached out and touched her arm. "I should warn you, Rose. He may not be the same man you once knew."

✦

Rose was alarmed by what she saw. Liam's face was very pale, almost sheet-white. The scar above his eye was more vivid than she remembered. At least he was sleeping, although fitfully. She desperately wanted to hold his hand but refrained for fear of waking him. Instead, she whispered, "I thank God, Liam, you're alive."

Suddenly, he became more agitated. Startled, Rose reached out and placed a hand on his shoulder, in an attempt to calm him. He started to speak, at first unintelligibly, but then his words became clear. "Stay down, Dieter!" he cried out. "Keep your head down!"

Rose shook his shoulder, trying to wake him up. "It's just a nightmare, Liam. It's all right."

Liam's eyes opened. What Rose now saw unnerved her. His face had taken on the tormented look of a man in the iron grip of some terrible demon.

"It's all right, Liam. It's Rose. I'm here."

"Rose? Is it you?"

"Yes, Liam, it's me."

"I didn't recognize him at first, Rose … almost four years since I last saw him …"

"Who, Liam? Who's Dieter?"

"Ja-sus, Rose, he died right before my eyes."

Rose felt a hand on her shoulder. It was Edith. "We should let him rest, Rose. You look like you could use some sleep, too. Why don't you come back in the morning?"

Reluctantly, Rose left and returned to her dormitory. In the morning she came back, only to find another wounded soldier in the bed Liam had occupied. Liam was on his way to Britain.

✦

In the days that followed the Battle of Moreuil Wood, the Germans renewed the efforts to capture Amiens. However, by this time, the British and the French had been able to bring up reinforcements and strengthen their defences. On April 5, the German high command abandoned Operation Michael. In three weeks of fighting the German army had suffered over three hundred thousand casualties. Amiens had been saved.

✦

Chapter 17

April 25, 1918

ROSE HURRIEDLY DRESSED. SHE'D SLEPT IN, AND BEING late was a serious offence, one her section leader didn't take lightly. It didn't matter that Rose's evacuation convoy to Boulogne the previous night didn't return to Etaples until the small hours of the morning. All drivers were expected to show up for roll call at seven-thirty a.m.

She rushed out the door of her hut and ran down the duckboard that led to the compound where the ambulances were parked. Halfway there she tripped on a loose plank and fell to her hands and knees. "Oh, damn!" she cried out.

"I have no' heard a lassie use that kind of language since I left home."

Rose looked up, prepared to get a scolding from some overbearing officer. Instead, she was greeted with a friendly grin and the offer of a helping hand from a corporal who introduced himself as Alex MacNeil. Home, he explained, was Alberta, Canada.

Rose was more interested in his cap badge. "You're with Lord Strathcona's Horse."

"Aye, miss. Know the Strathconas, do you?"

"Just one," Rose answered with a smile.

The corporal, it turned out, was visiting a friend in the hospital before heading to England on leave. They agreed to meet in an hour.

Overhead the sea gulls went about their daily business under the warm spring sun. Wisps of white cloud scudded by. Only the sound of a bugler playing the Last Post at a nearby cemetery reminded Rose and Alex that there was a war on.

"Off duty now?" Alex asked.

"Just for an hour," Rose replied. "I have to get back to my ambulance to have it ready for engine inspection at ten-thirty."

Nearby, two nursing sisters, out for a morning's walk, stopped and looked in their direction, looks of disapproval on their faces.

"Can you tell a lie, Corporal?"

"Anything for a pretty lass."

"If those two ask who you are, would you introduce yourself as my brother?"

"I understand. You're no' to be alone with a man without a chaperone."

"The Brits and their Victorian morality."

Alex laughed. "Well, I doubt you can fake a Scottish brogue. How about your brother-in-law?"

Rose smiled. "Agreed."

"You're the woman he met in London."

"Liam spoke of me?"

"Well, not very much. Liam's a wee bit shy when it comes to matters of the heart." Alex went on to say that he planned to visit Liam at the hospital north of London where he was convalescing.

"When you see him, would you tell him I send my love?"

"I would be happy to."

A strong breeze whistled through the boughs of a nearby stand of pines and ruffled the tufts of grass that dotted the sand dunes. "There's something else, Corporal, something I would like to know."

"What is it?" Alex asked.

"What happened that day when Liam was wounded?"

"Now there's a tale for the history books, if there ever was one."

Rose listened in awe as Alex told her about "C" Squadron's charge at Moreuil Wood. "Only one man survived unharmed," he said, bringing the story to a close. "A third of the men, including Lieutenant Flowerdew, were killed. Some of the wounded like Liam couldn't be reached until darkness. The Lieutenant's been awarded the Victoria Cross posthumously."

Rose had heard of Britain's highest honour for bravery.

"Saw a Victoria Cross once," Alex said. "Has but two words inscribed on it: 'For Valour.' Flowerdew certainly deserved it."

"And so, Corporal," Rose added, "did the men who went with him."

Alex nodded his agreement.

A hundred kilometres to the east, at a newly constructed airfield in German-occupied Belgium, a ground crew readied R.60 for a bombing mission that night. Finally, after three days of heavy rain and fog, the meteorologists had forecast a clear sky.

Paul Langer welcomed the busy routine of pre-flight preparation. It was far better than dwelling on the thought that had recently come to prey on his mind. Germany, Paul had concluded, was going to lose the war. The facts were undeniable. Four weeks had passed since the Emperor's Battle was launched, and so far a decisive victory had eluded Germany. Soon, the Americans would be joining the battle in full force. Paul had visited the United States on business trips. He had seen for himself the industrial might the Americans had built. There was no doubt in his mind that American power would give the British and the French the upper hand. Paul's loyalty to his country, however, remained unshaken. He would continue to do his duty right to the bitter end. He owed his son that much.

Since February 18, Paul had flown three more successful missions over Britain. Tonight, however, he had a new target. Since the start of the Emperor's Battle, the flow of enemy reinforcements from Britain through the French channel ports had increased dramatically. To disrupt this supply line, the German Supreme Command had turned to the R-planes stationed in Belgium. Tonight, R.60 would bomb the city of Boulogne.

Evacuation convoys from Etaples to Boulogne took three hours for a round trip. This night there were six ambulances in Rose's convoy. The drive to the French port was uneventful. It was on the return trip that things went wrong for Rose.

Just as the convoy was ready to leave the harbour, the lights of Boulogne were turned off as a precaution against air raids. These blackouts included vehicle headlights. Left to find their way out of the city in darkness, the ambulance drivers often became separated from their convoys. This time it was Rose's turn. By the time she reached the city's outskirts, the other drivers were nowhere in sight.

To make matters worse, halfway to Etaples, the front left tire of Rose's ambulance went flat. She braked to a stop, shut off the engine and reluctantly stepped down from the cab into the ankle-deep mud churned up by the constant traffic and the recent heavy rains. She switched on her flashlight and shone it on the deflated tire. Just a few days ago she'd patched a hole in its tube. Had the patch not held? Was it a fresh puncture? She couldn't believe her bad luck.

Rose looked towards Etaples, and then back to Boulogne, hoping to hear another vehicle approaching, but the road was deserted. She stared again at the flat tire. Her ambulance was equipped with demountable rims, each secured to its wheel by six wedge bolts. Stored in the back was a fully inflated spare mounted on its own rim. To use the spare, however, Rose would have to crawl underneath the ambulance and jack up the wheel. She took one look at the foul-smelling muck and felt her stomach turn.

Then she heard the familiar report of anti-aircraft guns. She looked back to the night sky over Boulogne, now lit up by searchlights. An air raid meant casualties. Soon every ambulance would be needed. She trudged to the toolbox mounted on the frame behind the cab and took out the wrench and the jack.

That night R.60 flew an indirect route to its target. After taking off, Paul headed west to the sea before turning south towards Boulogne. The plan was to avoid the strong enemy anti-aircraft defences east of the city and to gain the element of surprise. However, as he approached Boulogne, Paul discovered that the city's defenders were on the alert.

It wasn't long before searchlights locked on R.60, bringing a concentrated fire from the anti-aircraft guns below. Inside the cabin, Paul and his co-pilot gripped the steering controls as the bursts of shrapnel rocked the huge aircraft. They were determined to keep R.60 on course until its load of eighteen one-hundred-kilogram high explosive bombs was released. Then they would send the Giant into a dive to elude the searchlights.

But fate wouldn't co-operate. Just as the navigator released the last of the bombs, direct shrapnel hits started fires in both the starboard and port engines. Immediately, Paul reached behind the throttle controls and flipped the master ignition switch, shutting down all four engines. This quick action succeeded in extinguishing the fire in the port engines, but the starboard engines continued to burn. Through the window of the cockpit Paul could see the starboard mechanic enveloped in flame. Without power, R.60 quickly began to lose altitude.

Rose worked as quickly as she could. It had taken all her strength to loosen the nuts on the wedge bolts that held the deflated tire and its rim in place. Now came the more daunting job of jacking up the wheel. Spurred on by the sound of exploding bombs, she dropped to her knees in the mud next to the driver's door, holding the flashlight in one hand, the jack in the other. Then she lowered herself to her elbows and crawled underneath the front fender in behind the wheel, her face just centimetres from the fetid muck. The stench was overwhelming, causing her to retch, but she willed herself to go on. Her leather trench coat gave her some protection, but the slime soon saturated her stockings and oozed into her boots.

Rose positioned the jack near the wheel and, using the shaft of the wrench as a handle, ratcheted the leg up until the saddle was snug under the axle. She continued working the handle until the base of the jack found a firm footing under the mud and the wheel began to rise. Once it turned freely, she pushed herself out from under the ambulance, banging her head on the running board as she tried to keep her face clear of the muck.

On her feet, Rose rubbed her bruised head and looked down at the mud slithering down the front of her coat. She didn't know whether to laugh or cry. Instead, she was suddenly startled out of her wits by a huge burning object that passed just overhead with a loud swoosh. In the light of the flames she could make out the shape of an aircraft. Within seconds there was a loud crash.

Rose froze where she stood, staring into the night in disbelief. A large aircraft — it had to be an enemy bomber! Her first instinct was to go for help. But how? Until the tire was changed, the ambulance was of no use. Then she heard men shouting and saw flames leap into the sky.

R.60's slow speed of descent had reduced the force of the impact, allowing the crew in the cabin to escape the wreckage with only minor injuries. The mechanics flying in the outer cockpits weren't so fortunate. Only Hans survived the crash. While the crew tended to his injuries, Paul stood and watched the fire consume the wreckage of his aircraft. Soon enemy soldiers would arrive to take them prisoner. At least R.60's highly classified equipment wouldn't fall into their hands.

"Captain Langer!" the co-pilot called out. "Come quickly!"

Paul turned and ran to his crew huddled a short distance away.

"It's Hans, Captain. A shell fragment's severed the artery in his upper leg. We've tied a bootlace around his leg as a tourniquet, but he's still bleeding. If he doesn't get medical help soon, he'll die."

The mechanic cried out in pain. Paul knelt down beside him, gripping his hand tightly in his own. "Hold on, Hans," he said. "Enemy soldiers'll be here any minute."

"Captain," the co-pilot interrupted, "we have a visitor."

Paul glanced over his shoulder. What he saw brought him quickly to his feet. Standing in the light of the fire was a woman, wearing a cap and a trench coat. Pulled up above the peak of her cap was a pair of goggles.

Her coat, skirt and boots were caked in mud.

"Who are you?" he asked in German.

The woman didn't answer. Instead, she pushed passed him, knelt down by Hans and looked at his wound.

Paul reached out and grabbed her arm. "Are you a nurse?" he demanded, this time in English.

The woman turned her head and stared at him, unflinching. "I'm an American serving as an ambulance driver with the Voluntary Aid Detachment. Now, if you want this man to live, you'll stand aside."

Paul let go of her arm and moved away. With the rest of his crew he watched, dumbfounded, while the woman unbuttoned Hans' trousers. Then, with both her thumbs, she applied pressure to a point in his lower abdomen on the side of the wounded leg about the width of a hand from his hip. Within seconds, the bleeding subsided.

"Now retie that tourniquet," she ordered the copilot who promptly did as he was told.

"Captain," another crewman called out, "enemy soldiers are here!"

The woman stood up and fixed Paul with the same fearless stare. The hatred in her eyes bore through him like two hot coals. "I applied pressure to the femoral artery," she said. "I've learned a few things working around doctors and nurses."

Before he could reply, she turned on her heels and walked away.

✦

In the four months following Operation Michael, the German High Command launched four more attacks in the west. Although they succeeded in creating huge bulges in the British and French lines, none of these attacks achieved a breakthrough. The enemy simply had too many men. Germany, on the other hand, lacked the manpower to replace the hundreds of thousands of German soldiers who had been killed, wounded or taken prisoner. With the failure of the Emperor's Battle, all hope of ever forcing Britain and France to ask for peace on Germany's terms was gone.

By August 1918, the British and the French, bolstered by the Americans, were ready to seize the initiative. Major assaults, spearheaded by the Canadians and Australians, were launched all along the Western Front. By October the German defences had been breached. Britain and France were now in a position to demand that Germany surrender on their terms. Germany had no choice but to accept. The war came to an end on November 11.

✦

Chapter 18

December 11, 1918

Lili Bloch visited Freiburg's cathedral as she did every morning before heading off to her first piano lesson. At the altar she lit a candle, then knelt to pray. The candle was for Dieter Hannsen, the prayer for Germany.

The end of the war had given Germans more reason to pray than to rejoice. The victors were in no mood to be merciful. Germany, in their judgement, had caused the war, and Germany would have to pay a heavy price. Their demands would be set down in a peace treaty which Germany would be required to sign. Until this was done, the British blockade would remain in force.

Germany now faced another winter of hunger. To help put food on their table, Ernst had been forced to join the growing number of beggars on the streets of Freiburg. As if this weren't enough, Germany was on the brink of civil war, as opposing political forces prepared for an armed struggle to take control of the government.

This morning Lili had another reason to ask God for guidance. The previous day she had witnessed from the window of her flat an incident that left her badly shaken. A gang of youths had attacked an elderly Jewish man in the street below. Anti-Semitism was rearing its ugly head as some sought scapegoats to blame for Germany's misery. When the attackers scattered at the sound of a police whistle, Lili had got a good look at one of them. It was Dieter's nephew, Tomas Kaufmann.

Lili had lain awake that night, agonizing over what to do. Should she inform Tomas' mother of what she'd seen? Was it her place to do so? If only Dieter were alive. He would know what to do.

✦

At that same moment, a cold, damp wind blew in from the Celtic Sea and swept over Ireland's Old Head of Kinsale as it had done for eons. Rose and Liam left the motorcar they'd rented near the lighthouse and walked over to the cliff's edge. The heavy waves broke against the rocks below. On the horizon dark clouds threatened a winter storm.

Almost four years had passed since that bright spring day when the locals had come to the Old Head for an afternoon's outing in the warm sunshine. Instead, they'd watched in horror as the *Lusitania* disappeared beneath the sea. Rose and Liam now stood on the same spot.

Nearly twelve hundred people had drowned that day. Among them were Mary Kincaid, age thirty-five, her daughter Elizabeth, age ten, and son James, age four. Of the three, only James's body had been recovered. He was buried in a mass grave in a cemetery in Queenstown.

For the longest while, Rose stared at the angry sea. Finally, Liam put his arm around her shoulder and drew her close to him. "It's time, Rose," he said, "time to say goodbye."

She could no longer hold back the tears. "I'm so sorry, Mary," she sobbed, "I did all I could for Liza. I would've gladly died in her place."

The wind, raw and piercing, suddenly howled, tearing at their clothing. "We should go now, Rose," Liam urged. "That storm is blowin' up quick."

They set out for Queenstown in silence. At the wheel, Liam concentrated on the winding, narrow road ahead, while Rose gazed out the passenger window at the rugged Irish countryside. The fact was they'd hardly spoken a word to each other during their short stay in Ireland. It was Rose's decision to prolong her stay in Europe that had driven a wedge between them.

Finally, she could stand the silence no longer. "Liam,

we'll only be separated for six months," she tried to reason. "Then I'll come to Ottawa, and we can start a new life together like we've planned."

Liam answered without taking his eyes off the road. "It's not the time we'll be apart, Rose, that bothers me. It's you I worry about. You've got to start puttin' the war behind you. Workin' with refugee children in Belgium for the American Red Cross is not goin' to help. It'll only make it harder to forget. The sooner we put the ocean between us and this godforsaken continent, the better. Let the Europeans fight their own damn battles. That's why I want you to come with me when the Strathconas sail home in the spring."

She didn't want to argue with him anymore. But she was also determined not to give in. "It's something I must do Liam. Please try to understand. It'll be the best thing for me."

"I hope you're right, Rose. I just hope you're right."

Rain started to fall, large drops splattering the windscreen. Their vehicle was equipped with a manual wiper, which Liam began to operate by sliding a lever back and forth with his free hand. Ahead they could see the lights of Queenstown where they could find shelter before the brunt of the storm hit.

Liam's return to Canada came sooner than expected. A month later he wrote to Rose to tell her that he'd just received word that his mother had died. The devastating epidemic of Spanish flu that was terrorizing Europe had spread to North America. Maeve Cassidy had been one of its victims. He went on to explain that he had applied for and received a special leave to return to Canada. His ship would sail from England on the last day of January.

Liam was going home.

✦

For the 1918-1919 season the National Hockey League had three teams: the Toronto Arenas, the Montreal Canadiens and the Ottawa Senators. The Canadiens defeated the Senators in a best-of-seven playoff for the right to travel west to play the Seattle Metropolitans of the Pacific Coast Hockey League for the Stanley Cup. With the series tied at two wins each, tragedy struck. Many of the players were stricken with the Spanish flu. When one of the players died, the series was cancelled.

The NHL looked forward to the 1919-1920 season. Joining Ottawa, Montreal and Toronto, whose team was now called the St. Patricks, was a team from Quebec City. The end of the war saw the return of players who had served overseas and brought the promise of bigger crowds.

✦

Chapter 19

December 13, 1919

JIMMY MULLEN AND HIS FATHER GOT OFF THE STREETCAR on Laurier Avenue and joined the throng of people heading for the main entrance to Dey's Arena, home of the Ottawa Senators. To some Ottawans, the box-like arena was an eyesore; in Jimmy's imagination, it was a palace. This was the ten-year-old's first Senators game, an early Christmas gift from his father, and he was bursting with excitement. Tonight the Senators hosted the Toronto St. Pats. The game had been sold out for weeks.

Jimmy joined the capacity crowd of seventy-five hundred spectators in a resounding cheer as the teams skated on to the ice for the opening face-off. By the end of the first period, the young boy had found a hero, a speedy winger, who had scored one of Ottawa's two goals.

"What's his name?" Jimmy asked his father.

"That's Liam Cassidy. He's just back from overseas. The team was worried that his war injuries might have slowed him down a bit. But he doesn't seem to have lost a step."

"Can I get his autograph after the game?"

"We'll see," replied his father.

Liam was one of the last players to leave the dressing room.

"Sorry to keep you waitin'," he said to Jimmy as he wrote his name on the back of an envelope the boy's father had found in his coat pocket. "I'm not used to doin' this."

"You'd better get used to it," Jimmy's father said,

shaking Liam's hand. "Good game."

"Yeah, good game, Liam," said Jimmy, an adoring look on his face.

"Thanks," Liam replied.

They began walking together towards the main entrance. "I'm still gettin' used to making forward passes between those two blue lines. That new rule sure changes the way the game is — "

That's when Liam noticed her, standing just inside the main doors. A year had passed since he last saw her. He stood still, captivated by her smile, as he had been that day on the steamer out of Boulogne.

"I apologize, Liam, for being late," Rose said. "Did you get my telegram?"

He shook his head. "When you didn't arrive on the afternoon train, I just figured you'd changed your mind."

"I'm so sorry, Liam. I missed my connection in New York City and had to wait for the next train."

Liam turned to Jimmy and put a hand on his shoulder. "Remember to practise, lad. There's no glory in this game without hard work."

Jimmy and his father thanked him and said goodbye, leaving them alone.

"You're more beautiful than I remember, Rose."

"Well, aren't you the forward one, Liam Cassidy."

Eddie Gerard, the Senators' captain, appeared on his way out the door. Liam introduced him to Rose.

"Will you be in Ottawa for long, Miss Pearce?" Eddie asked.

"It depends," Rose answered, looking at Liam.

Sensing that his presence wasn't welcomed, Eddie said good night and headed for the door. As he opened it, he looked back and said, "Liam, are you sure you want to sell that rifle of yours?"

"Yeah, I'm sure," Liam replied.

"Then I'll be by in the morning to have a look at it." With that, he gave a wave and disappeared into the night, leaving them alone once again.

It was Rose who spoke first. "You're planning to purchase a new hunting rifle?"

"No," Liam replied. "I just want to get rid of the one I have. I've seen enough rifles for one lifetime, Rose. I'm just tryin' to put the war behind me. I was hopin' you'd say the same."

She moved closer to him, taking his hands in hers. "The war has also left me with ghosts, Liam, ghosts that will continue to haunt me for the rest of my life. But there's something else you must understand. I'm a person in my own right, capable of doing anything I put my mind to."

Liam gently squeezed her hands and smiled. "I'm used to having a strong woman in my life."

She laughed and threw her arms around his neck. Liam held her tightly, not wanting to let go. Rose seemed to sense his uneasiness. "I'm here to stay, Liam," she said. "All I want is a life with you."

The taxi pulled up to the entrance of the Chateau Laurier, the city's new luxury hotel. Liam asked the driver to wait while he saw Rose into the lobby. As the hotel doorman helped Rose out of the cab, he said to Liam, "Good evening, Mr. Cassidy. I hear the Senators won tonight's match." Liam walked by him without a reply. He didn't care much for hotel doormen.

Nor would he ever get used to the grandeur of luxury hotels. Standing in the lobby of the Chateau Laurier, Liam felt completely out of place. Rose seemed to sense his discomfort. "Liam, I want very much to see the city you know. Will you show me tomorrow?"

"Are you sure, Rose? My world isn't London or

Boston. I don't want to disappoint you."

"Would I've come all this way, Liam, if I didn't want to be part of your world?"

Liam smiled. "No, I suppose not. I'll come by after lunch then, around one, if that's okay?"

"One o'clock would be fine."

"You'd better get something warmer to wear."

Rose laughed. "I'm afraid I didn't come prepared for the Canadian winter."

Liam wanted very much to kiss Rose again but held back, wondering if displays of affection between a man and woman were allowed in the Chateau Laurier's lobby. Rose, however, didn't hesitate. She kissed him tenderly and wished him a good night.

The taxi driver dropped Liam at his mother's house on Queen Street West. He hung his coat in the vestibule and went into the kitchen where he tended to a fire in the woodstove. He was about to head upstairs to bed when he stopped and looked at an envelope sitting on the kitchen table. It had come that morning in the mail. Liam sat down at the table, took a letter from the envelope and began to read it again. It was dated October 25, 1919.

Dear Mr. Cassidy,

Thank you for your letter. It took some time for it to reach us. It is only since the signing of the Versailles Peace Treaty that postal service between Germany and the outside world has begun to return to normal.

I am the sister of Albert Hannsen, Karl and Dieter's father. I am writing to you on behalf of my brother who passed away shortly af-

ter your letter arrived. This letter is not in my handwriting but rather that of an acquaintance who was kind enough to translate my words into English.

The loss of both of his sons to the war was too much for my brother to bear. In the end his heart simply gave out. The burden he carried to his grave was made heavier by the knowledge that he had failed Dieter as a father. He had been so consumed by his grief over the death of one son that he had forgotten that he had another who needed his love. Learning from your letter that Dieter had died honourably, trying to save a life rather than take one, helped to ease his pain.

To make amends, my brother offered to help a young woman, a talented pianist, whom Dieter had befriended during his last leave. Before he died, Albert was able to use his influence to secure her a teaching position at the Freiburg Conservatory. Hopefully, she and her disabled brother can make their way in these uncertain times.

The outcome of the war has left Germany a deeply embittered nation. Hatred is rearing its ugly head. Already it has one of my children in its clutches.

I can only pray that this discontent will pass and that Germany will come to live with the rest of the world in peace and harmony.

Sincerely,
Ingrid Kaufmann

Liam turned his head to look at the Springfield cradled in its wall rack. Ever since returning from overseas, he'd thought about selling it. After reading Ingrid Kaufmann's letter that morning, he'd finally made up his mind. The rifle had become a daily reminder of the war, of the men he'd killed and of the friends who had died.

Liam's attention shifted to a nearby rocking chair. There was never a day when he didn't think of his mother. He got up from the table and went to a nearby cupboard. He opened the door, took out a bottle of Irish whiskey and poured some into a glass. He glanced once more at the rocking chair. "I'm sorry, Mum," he said softly, "but I need one drink to help me through the night. Just one."

Liam downed the whiskey in one swallow, set the glass down and climbed the stairs to his bedroom where he undressed and got into bed. The alcohol, he hoped, would help him drift off into dreamless sleep.

But, as always, it didn't.

Before long, the grisly image resurfaced.

Of Dieter Hannsen's head exploding in a spray of blood, bone and tissue as the marksman's bullet struck him in the face.

The new day broke with a cloudless sky. In the southeast, the sun slowly made its mid-December appearance, offering little warmth to raise the frigid temperature. Winter had come early to the Ottawa Valley, and the city had already dug itself out of two heavy snowfalls.

After breakfast, Rose spoke to the hotel manager about purchasing some winter clothing. He recommended a shop on Sparks Street that would be happy to deliver whatever she needed to the hotel. The parcels arrived just before lunch. They contained a heavy woolen coat and fleece-lined boots, as well as leather gloves and some winter underwear. Rose was ready in her new attire when Liam arrived an hour later. As they stepped out into the frosty air, she exclaimed, "Is it always this cold?"

"You'll get used to it," Liam replied. "It makes you appreciate the summers more."

"You mean you actually have summers in Canada!"

Liam chuckled at her joke. It was good to hear him laugh, Rose thought. At the arena the night before she'd sensed that he was still tormented by memories of the war. Whatever the future held for them, of one thing Rose was now certain: she would have to be strong, not only for herself, but for Liam as well. Taking hold of his arm, she asked, "Where are we going first?"

"To Parliament Hill. It's just up ahead."

As they walked up Wellington Street, the snow squeaking under their boots, Liam told her about the fire of 1916 that had gutted the Parliament Building. "What was left," he explained, "was beyond repair. So they tore it down and rebuilt it from scratch."

As the new Parliament Building came into view, Rose was impressed by what she saw. The parliamentary grounds rose gently from the street. On the height of land about three hundred metres away stood a magnificent stone building. "How did the fire start?" she asked as they stopped for a better look.

"There was a lot of talk at the time of German saboteurs," Liam replied, "but that's all it was, just talk. A government investigation decided it was an accident."

At the centre of the building, rising from the rear, was an elaborately decorated cone-shaped structure. "What's that?" Rose asked.

"That's the roof of the parliamentary library. It was the only part they managed to save from the fire. One day soon you won't be able to see it from here. In the spring they'll start buildin' a new tower at the front, much taller than the original one. It's to be called the Peace Tower, in memory of those who died in the war."

"Your country made a great sacrifice."

"Over sixty thousand killed, Rose, and many more, their bodies … their minds … crippled for life."

Rose felt Liam's body tremble. She put her arm around his waist and held him with all her strength. "I know, my love," she said, "I know."

Just then they heard the clanging of a bell. They turned to find a streetcar approaching.

"Let's take a ride," Liam said. "It's too cold to walk."

Le Breton Flats, Rose soon discovered, was a small residential and industrial community nestled between the river and the high ground which formed the heart of the city. The first thing she noticed, stepping off the streetcar, was the smell of rotten eggs. "What's that awful odour?" she asked.

"That's sulphur. It's coming from the Eddy paper mill," Liam explained, pointing to a tall smokestack by the river. "Come on," he said, taking her hand, "I'll show you where I live."

They headed north towards the river. The street they were on, Liam explained, was named after J. R. Booth, one of the city's lumber barons. The vast lumberyard off to their right was part of his empire. "I work for Mr. Booth when I'm not playin' hockey." Liam paused, then added, "He pays well."

What he meant, Rose understood, but was too proud to say, was that he had the means to support her. She knew that a life with Liam would not have all the material comforts she'd been used to. But being with the man she loved, she had decided, was far more important to her. "I know you'll be a good provider, Liam," she assured him.

At the first intersection, they turned left onto Queen Street West. At the corner was a grocery. Next to it was restaurant. The third building had four row houses. Liam stopped at the door to the first one. "Well, here it is," he said, climbing the steps. "How about a cup of hot coffee?"

"That's a grand idea, Liam."

Liam hung up their coats in the small vestibule and showed her into the parlour. In one corner was a small coal-burning stove. Liam opened the damper in the stovepipe and then removed the lid on top. With a poker he stoked what was left of the morning fire and then added some lumps of coal from a nearby box. "That should warm things up," he said. "Why don't you make yourself at home, Rose, while I put on the coffee pot." Then he disappeared into the back of the house, leaving her alone.

The parlour, Rose could see, was plainly decorated and simply furnished. There were three wooden chairs and a small sofa that was showing its wear. In another corner a gramophone sat on a table. What interested Rose was a framed photograph hanging on the opposite wall below a crucifix. She stepped across the room to get a closer look. It was a portrait of a young man and woman taken, she guessed, sometime before the turn of the century. The man stood, while the woman was seated on a chair in front of him.

At that moment Liam reappeared and came to her side. "Me dad and mum," he said. "It was taken just before they left Ireland. It was one of the few things Mum managed to save from the fire." He turned and put his hands gently on her shoulders. "I just wish, Rose, she could be here now to meet you."

She leaned forward and kissed his cheek. "Your mother must have been very proud of you, Liam."

"Why don't we have our coffee in the kitchen," he said. "There's somethin' I want to tell you."

They sat at the kitchen table by the warmth of the wood stove. Rose listened as Liam told her about Dieter Hannsen, a young German whom he befriended the winter before the war and who had died in France trying to save his life. So this was the man, she thought, whose name he'd called out in his delirium at the hospital in Etaples.

When he finished, Liam handed her an envelope. "It came yesterday," he said.

Rose noted the German postmark and stamp. She opened the envelope and took out the letter.

"I want you to read it," Liam said.

When she finished, she handed it back to him without a word.

"They were decent people, Rose, the professor and his sons. They would never have condoned what happened to the *Lusitania*."

When she finally spoke, there was anger in her voice. "But it did happen, Liam. All those innocent women and children were murdered."

"The war was an ugly business, Rose. Nothin' good came of it, only cemeteries."

And hate, Rose thought to herself. For four years a burning hatred for Germans had festered inside her. Liam seemed to be reading her mind. "You can't go on hatin', Rose."

He was right, of course. Rose knew it was unfair to condemn all Germans for what happened to the *Lusitania*. Ingrid Kaufmann's letter was proof that there were people of goodwill in Germany. "I'm very sorry," she said, "that your friend died."

"Rose, I don't want our sons to have to face another war."

"Nor our daughters, Liam."

"Nor them," he said.

They finished their coffee in silence. While Liam washed out their cups, Rose glanced out the kitchen window. Daylight was quickly fading.

"How about some supper," Liam suggested. "I'm not much for cookin', but we can get a decent meal next door."

"I'd like that."

Liam helped her on with her coat before putting on his. Outside they were greeted by the sound of children playing in the street to their left. About a dozen young boys, using a lump of coal for a puck, were engaged in a spirited game of hockey on a patch of ice left by a burst water main. One of the boys looked their way and called out to the others, "Look, it's Liam!" They all stopped and waved to him. "Good game last night, Liam!" another boy shouted.

"Thanks," Liam replied.

He turned to Rose. "I'm goin' to build us a house on a lot big enough for a rink in the backyard, so our boys won't have to play in the street."

All Rose could think of at the moment was the foul smell of sulphur that clung to the cold winter air. "Where will our house be?" she asked hesitatingly.

"There's good land for sale to the west along the river." Then he paused, with a twinkle in his eye. "And it's upwind from Eddy's."

Rose made no attempt to hide her relief. "A house to the west," she replied, "would definitely be a good idea."

They laughed together.

Acknowledgements

A number of books were consulted in my research. One that needs to be mentioned is *The German Giants: German R-Planes, 1914-1918* by G.W. Haddow and P.M. Grosz.

I am grateful to Father Raymond Vickers and Warrant Officer Darryl Crowell MB CD, Curator of the Lord Strathcona's Horse (Royal Canadians) Museum for their helping hands along the way.

Special thanks go to Captain Mike Calnan, instructor in the Royal Canadian Artillery and Curator of the Swords and Ploughshares Museum.

Finally, I want to express my deepest gratitude to my family — to my mother, to Steve, Gillian, Ryan, Randy and Dinah, and to my darling wife Barbara — without whose support and encouragement this project would never have reached fruition.